"What do you think  Pirate Hunter and the Spi

Weston furrowed his a wall?"

"No, behind a butterscotch sundae. How many ways are there to be immured? Yes, behind a brick wall."

"That's your idea...immursion?"

"Well, that's the start of my idea. By the by, 'immursion' isn't a word."

"By the by, faux-professor, you say 'by the by' an awful lot. I find all the 'by the bying' repetitive and repetitive. So what's the rest of it then...your idea?"

"Well, it's inchoate at present, but I thought there might be something in there worth exploring."

"Behind the wall?"

H.P. shook his head. "No, in that moment. I mean it's such a timeworn trope, but I thought we could approach it from a new angle. You know how much our characters like to prattle on. What would they say to someone immuring them?"

"Please stop?"

"Okay, so I take it you don't like this idea either."

"I didn't say that, but I'm not sure I understand where you're coming from. Shouldn't we be concerned with who's immuring them, why they're being immured, and how they'll ultimately escape their immuration rather than what they'll chat about while it's happening?"

Immurdered: Some Time to Kill

by

Wesley Payton

Downstate Illinois, Book 2

Immurdered: Some Time to Kill

Cover Art by *Debbie Taylor*

The Wild Rose Press, Inc.
PO Box 708
Adams Basin, NY 14410-0708
Visit us at www.thewildrosepress.com

Publishing History
First Edition, 2022
Trade Paperback ISBN 978-1-5092-3915-3
Digital ISBN 978-1-5092-3916-0

Downstate Illinois, Book 2
Published in the United States of America

Dedication

For Ralph "Bud" Edwards,
an exceptional coach who always taught
the importance of playing the game loosey-goosey.

Prologue

At a table in a campus café.

"If you expect me to coauthor a book with you, we're not using one of your asinine, alliterative *Spinster* titles," said H.P.

"Of course not," replied Weston. "This would be a different type of story altogether."

"Okay, just so long as the title isn't too punning…no excessive wordplay—that gets old fast and sets the wrong tone from the start."

"Sure, makes sense."

"And let's go easy on the meta elements," added H.P. "It's so overdone these days—a little meta goes a long way."

"Agreed."

"Also, we both tend to write a lot of dialogue, so we'd have to be careful not to get too carried away with that."

"Shakespeare wrote a lot of dialogue, and people still read his work," said Weston.

"Yes, but he was a playwright, and we're novelists. See, I know the difference because I also happen to be an instructor of creative writing."

"Well faux-professor, in case you've forgotten, Shakespeare was also a poet."

"Since he didn't write dialogue in his poetry, and

since neither of our prose is likely to be mistaken for the Bard's verse, I don't believe that's germane to this discussion."

"Then I take it that you see yourself as Herr Arbiter of germaneness for our little project."

"*Jawohl*," said H.P. "Someone needs to keep our story grounded. Sometimes when I read your stuff, like when I'm having trouble falling asleep, I don't even know where the characters are half the time—just talking heads floating in space."

"What does it matter where they are if what they're saying is interesting? Hamlet's soliloquy works as well on an empty stage as it does in a Denmarkian castle."

"But the play itself is what gives the soliloquy context…the actors, the choices made by the director, and the set—even if it's just bare boards under a spotlight. Minimalism is not the same as nothingness. When you give the reader dialogue without bothering to set the scene, then the whiteness on the page becomes the context, so really what you've given them is nothing at all. By the by, dumbass, 'Denmarkian' isn't a word. Danish is the adjective you should've used."

"That doesn't sound right," said Weston. "Danish castle makes me think of something out of Candyland."

"You're a child trapped in a middle-aged man's body, aren't you?"

"Same with Danish people—now I'm imagining a woman with pastries for breasts."

"No. People from Denmark are called Danes."

"That doesn't work either, because now I'm thinking of a man with a dog's face," Weston replied, "though that could be because I'm sitting across from you."

"Yeah, this collaboration is really off to a great start."

Chapter 1

Slim tried to stretch out his long legs in the squad car, but the sedan just didn't have the legroom of his half-ton pickup, nor did it offer the same command driving position. He figured he could see a lot farther down the road if he were sitting up higher in his truck, but then there wasn't so very much to see parked alongside a country intersection at midnight. A farmer who lived nearby had called the station to report that a car had raced past his house three times that night, which was what qualified as a hot tip now that summer was over. Slim thought it was probably some little old lady in a station wagon who'd gotten lost on her way home from bingo, but in the off chance it was a drag racer, or more likely a drunk driver, he'd parked behind a billboard for the local bait shop and waited, feeling every bit the cliché of a small-town cop.

Slim hadn't been waiting long when a coupe sped past at better than twice the posted speed limit, completely disregarding the stop sign at the crossroads. Slim hit the red and blues and peeled out, but at the rate of speed the sporty car was motoring, he didn't figure he had much chance of catching up in his cruiser. However, to Slim's surprise, the pursuit was short-lived; the Mustang quickly pulled over onto the gravel shoulder of the two-lane road. Slim parked behind it and ran the plate. The small computer screen informed him that the timeworn Mustang was registered—not surprisingly—to a man whose name was familiar to local law enforcement, though Slim had never had the pleasure of meeting him personally. Also unsurprisingly, the car's owner received two DUIs in the last eight months and currently had a suspended license. Slim exited his patrol car.

The driver had his arms out the window, using his left hand to smoke a cigarette. "Evening, Officer."

Slim approached the vehicle. "We're on the morning side of midnight now. You have any idea how fast you were going?"

"Speedometer's busted, but I reckon in the low triple digits."

"That sounds about right." Slim shined his flashlight into the Mustang. "What happened…get kicked out of your regular bar, so you thought it'd be a good idea if you and Joe Six-Pack riding shotgun there turned the night into a mobile party?"

"He was Joseph Twelve-Pack when I first picked him up, but a fella gets thirsty driving around so fast."

"What's your deal—you like getting arrested or something?"

"How many lights you got on that thing anyway?" The driver pointed back at Slim's squad car, ignoring the question put to him. "For a minute there, I thought I was getting pulled over by a damn spaceship. I bet your cop car has more lights on the outside than my trailer has on the inside."

Slim followed the driver's gaze to the strobing lights on his squad car. "Well, I'll tell you what, I'll let you count those lights on your way to jail."

"I'm not going to jail, Officer."

"How do you figure?" Slim looked back down at the driver, realizing that the bright lights had momentarily ruined his eyes' natural night vision.

"Because you was wrong before," the driver called out. "My beer is riding in the passenger seat, but my shotgun is riding in the trunk."

The Mustang's trunk lid popped up faster than Slim could unholster his sidearm and pivot toward the rear of the vehicle. The muzzle flash from the shotgun obscured the face of the gunman who fired it. Then all Slim could see was darkness, and all he could hear was squealing tires and an endlessly echoing bang.

Chapter 2

Weston held his seven-month-old daughter at the kitchen table as Becky, Lance, and Vance buzzed around, preparing lunches for the day. He talked to her in a babyish voice as she grabbed at his nose. "Who has the worst name ever? You do. That's right, you do."

"I've asked you repeatedly not to tease the baby about her name." Becky stood over him with a jar of peanut butter and a dull knife held menacingly.

"It's just so awful that I want to prepare her for all the ridicule she'll undoubtedly be subjected to for years to come."

"If anyone makes fun of her name, she can explain its beautiful meaning."

"It's Hebrew for 'grace,' " Lance added.

"I am aware. I was there in the delivery room ardently objecting when your mother chose it. Incidentally, the name 'Grace' is English for 'grace.' "

"Her name's not so bad," Van said. "We can call her 'An' for short...like how people call me 'Van' instead of Vance."

"First of all," Weston began. " 'Van' is an automobile and 'An' is an article, neither of which are suitable names for humans. Secondly, both your names are monosyllabic, so there's no reason to shorten them."

Lance rolled his eyes. "It's been like half a year...probably time you got over it. Names aren't that big a deal, or do you think that's *Not Sew*?"

"You just said my name backward, didn't you?" asked Weston. "Clever, though it's the wrong 'sew' word."

" 'Sew' sue me." Lance noticed the jar in his mom's hand. "You're not making me a peanut butter sandwich, are you?"

"Of course, you love PB&Js."

"I told you my school started a no-peanuts policy this year…I can't wait to go to junior high next year."

Becky raised her arms in exasperation. "What am I supposed to make then? I can't make you a lunchmeat sandwich because it's going to sit inside your backpack getting sweaty all morning, and I can't make you a cheese sandwich because you won't eat any cheese that doesn't come on a pizza."

"What about just a jelly sandwich?" Lance asked.

"I might as well send you with a five-pound bag of sugar. You'll be bouncing off your classroom walls all afternoon."

"Throw in some salty potato chips," Weston suggested. "It'll even him out."

"Yeah," said Lance.

Becky looked at Lance. "Nope." Then turned to Weston. "And not helping."

Lance opened the refrigerator door. "I'll find some leftovers."

"Find some veggies instead—there should be carrots in the fridge." Becky looked at the clock on the stove. "Come on, guys, we need to leave like now. Weston, you sure you don't want me to drop you off at the hospital…it's on the way to the high school?"

"My appointment's not until ten, and I don't want

to spend any more time in that waiting room than I have to."

Van sat down next to Weston. "You know, I believe colonoscopies are called procedures—not appointments. Are you nervous about them having a looksee up the old tailpipe?"

Becky glowered at Vance. "Vancy, don't tease Weston about his procedure...I mean appointment."

"Why not? He was teasing my baby sister."

"Yes, but men his age are more sensitive than babies."

"Okay, I won't tease him about his colonoscopy." Van turned back to Weston. "So are you worried that when you get to the hospital, they'll find something else wrong with you and just decide to keep you there for good."

"I'm old enough that that's not funny."

"They say that tragedy plus time equals comedy, and I figure it'll only take a few minutes for me to find the humor in it."

"I really hope you get into college." Weston noticed Lance standing statue still in front of the open refrigerator. "Are you actively looking for something in there?"

"Carrots...or leftover pizza, both of which I think are on the top shelf."

"So your plan is to stand there with the fridge door open until you grow tall enough to reach them?"

"Never mind about the carrots." Becky folded over the top of his lunch bag. "I packed you an orange instead."

Lance closed the refrigerator door. "That's a fruit, not a vegetable."

"They're the same color, and we're in a hurry. Besides, you'll probably just end up trading it anyway. You boys grab your lunch bags off the counter and go on out to the Jeep. I'll take baby Ance."

Weston stood up and handed the little girl over to her mother. "Are you sure you don't want me to drop our unimaginatively named daughter off at daycare?"

"I want your morning to be as stress free as possible before your…appointment, and I know how much you loathe making small talk with the nuns."

"I feel like they're always judging me."

"That's what nuns do…it's part of their job description. Maybe if we were married, they wouldn't seem so judgmental."

"Or maybe they seem that way because you gave our Catholic kid a Jewish name."

"Possibly…something for you to ruminate over during your—"

"Tailpipe inspection?"

Becky kissed her baby's daddy. "Maybe later tonight I'll inspect your radiator hose."

Chapter 3

Despite his repeated attempts at dillydallying, Weston arrived ten minutes earlier than the appointed time for his procedure. *Where's a traffic obstructing train when you need one?* He walked past the waiting room entrance and perambulated down the hallway of the small hospital. He espied Mayor McCormick standing outside a recovery room at the end of the corridor, talking to a police officer. The mayor nodded at Weston when the officer left.

"How did you hear about Slim?" asked the mayor. "I haven't even released a statement yet."

"As I'm sure I've mentioned before, news travels fast in this small town."

"Well, you certainly appear to be plugged in...you seem more like of a local every time I see you."

"There's no reason to be insulting," said Weston. "So what's Slim's condition?"

"He's still unconscious; the doctors will be better able to assess his chances for making a complete recovery when he comes to. He was both lucky and unlucky. Near as we can ascertain, the assailant fired a deer slug from a 12-gauge shotgun at pointblank range, which kept the impact localized to his chest rather than if he'd been hit by buckshot; however, despite the slug hitting his bulletproof vest, it still made a hell of an impact, like getting kicked by a thoroughbred. The trauma caused deep contusions and an atrial fibrillation that led to what the docs characterized as a significant cardiac event. To make matters worse, he lay on the side of that desolate backroad for nearly an hour before the ambulance was able to reach him."

"Jesus…has anyone talked to his son yet?"

"The boy is staying with Slim's ex-wife now. I'm going over to see him after Slim wakes up and the docs can get a better read on his prognosis."

"What about this assailant?" Weston asked. "Is he in custody yet?"

"Maybe yes, maybe no. We've got the guy who owns the car Slim pulled over locked up at the police station. His name was the last search result on the computer in Slim's cruiser, and the tire tracks at the scene match the car registered to him. We found his car parked catawampus in his front yard, though to be fair it's difficult to tell with mobile homes what constitutes the front yard and what the driveway."

"That sounds like the yes part, so what's the no?"

"The no is it doesn't add up…at all. The idiot in lockup has a rap sheet longer than a summer's day, but it's all for things like driving while intoxicated and public urination—nothing violent. All of a sudden, he wants to give cop killing a try? There's got to be more to the story. What's also mystifying is that Slim's pistol was still holstered, and the supposed assailant had a BAC three times the legal limit when they found him passed out on the floor of his trailer. So this drunk that Slim pulled over got the drop on him at pointblank range with a long gun…doesn't make any sense."

"I know a little about arranging the details of a story so that they make sense," said Weston. "Is this guy talking yet?"

"Talking? He's babbling like a brook—mostly about how he blacked out and can't remember a damn thing from last night."

"Would you mind if I had a chat with him?"

"You know I can't give a civilian access to a suspect we have in custody for the attempted murder of a police officer."

"Incidentally, I thought your summer's day simile was pretty solid."

"I get it, you helped me by looking into my son's case when I asked you, and now you're asking me to let you help with Slim's case."

"But I don't think your babbling brook simile represents your best efforts."

"I hear you...okay fine, follow me down to the station, and I'll let you talk to—not interrogate—the suspect for five minutes. If anyone asks, you've taken a professional interest in this nascent investigation."

"Like maybe research for a new book?"

"Sure...though think more along the lines of Truman Capote than Nora Roberts."

Chapter 4

Weston entered the police station behind Mayor McCormick. He recognized the faces of some of the officers from the aftermath of the incident at the shooting club several months back. On rainy days, he still felt phantom pains in his foot from the toe he lost. The two walked past the front desk. "They've moved him to a conference room back here."

Weston thought the wood paneling on the walls imbued the station with a VFW hall vibe. "Cops have conferences?"

"As you might imagine, everybody's a little on edge this morning, so maybe take it easy with the wisecracks." They came to a stop in front a door to a small room with a big table.

"You bet...are you going to be behind a two-way mirror or something?"

"No, I'm going in the room with you so that I can ensure you don't brace the suspect and violate his civil rights."

"So good cop/bad cop then?"

"Absolutely not," said the mayor. "This is strictly a no cop/no cop, off-the-record chat."

"And there's no two-way mirror?"

"I told you, this is a conference room."

"That's disappointing. I was hoping someone could explain to me why they call it a two-way mirror…seems like it should be called a one-way mirror and one-way window."

"I'm pleased that you're taking this so seriously."

"Quipping is part of my process."

"Well your process better take all of five minutes." The mayor opened the door for Weston and then followed him in.

The mayor took a seat across from the suspect as Weston positioned himself near the window. The suspect studied him with bloodshot eyes. "Hey, you're that writer guy who moved here from the city awhile back, ain'tcha?"

Weston turned from the window to look at the suspect. "Who me?"

"Yeah, you write them Spinster books. My ex-wife had your *Soporific Spinster* on the nightstand the whole year we was married. She could never read more than a page or so before she fell asleep."

"I'm sorry to hear that your marriage didn't last."

"It lasted long enough. So you working on another book?"

"Always."

"You know, most people move away from small towns to find adventure…you're the first person I ever heard of who did it backward."

"What can I say, writing fiction books requires a novel approach."

The suspect chuckled. "That's funny…it's been a while since I had a laugh. So you think I might figure into one of your stories?"

"Maybe, though you'd have to tell me your story first."

"I was born just down the road a piece—"

"Pardon my interrupting, but I want to be respectful of your time." Weston twirled a finger in the air to indicate an accelerated pace. "Can you skip ahead to what happened last night?"

"I would if I could, but honestly I don't remember anything after I left the bar...not until the cops busted down my door this morning."

Weston crossed his arms. "What bar?"

"Well, it ain't got no name, but out front it's got a neon sign with—"

"Sorry again for the interruption, but that's the Boutonniere."

The suspect looked confused. "You sure about that?"

"Indeed I am, please continue."

"There's not much more to tell. I had...uh, a couple of beers...and then decided it best if I drove home before I got too inebriated."

"Did you talk with anyone at the bar?"

"Sure, I guess...I mean I ordered beer from the bartender, shot some pool with a guy in a cowboy hat—whipped him good too, and then I chatted with a pertty gal at the bar for a spell."

"As I'm sure you're aware, good writing is all about details. I've made the acquaintance of the bartender at the Boutonniere, but what can you tell me about the guy in the cowboy hat."

"Not much. We only played one game on account that I beat him so bad."

"You noticed his hat though...was it old or new?"

"New, I'd say."

"Was it dark or light?"

"It was a black hat."

"Did it look expensive or like it came from Walmart?"

"It was nice…maybe a Stetson."

"Okay, that's helpful." Weston rubbed his chin. "What about the gal?"

"What about her?"

"How 'pertty' was she? Like after a few beers she looked pretty because she was the only woman in the bar?"

"No, not like that…she was an honest to goodness knockout. I'd never seen her before, though I don't go to that bar very often."

"Why'd you go last night?"

"Change of scenery, I suppose. Besides, the bartenders at a couple of my usual places suggested that I branch out a bit more."

"What'd you and the knockout talk about?"

"Oh, this and that."

"So you talked about pronouns."

"Honestly, I don't remember what we talked about—all I remember was that she was good looking, and…"

"And?"

"And that she bought me a beer."

"I imagine a good-looking gal buying you a beer in a place like that would qualify as memorable…but then I should think that what happened next would likewise qualify."

"Yeah, what you're saying makes sense." The suspect looked up at Weston. "But I'm telling you…I just don't recall nothing after that."

The mayor cleared his throat. "Okay, that's all we have time for…I'm sure there are others who want to use this room."

"Wait, what do you think of my story…is there a book in it?"

Weston crossed the room. "If there is, so far it sounds rather open-and-shut, but then sometimes you don't get the full story until you read between the lines."

The mayor followed Weston into the hallway and closed the door behind him. "I've got to hand it to you, he told you as much in a few minutes as he did anyone else in the last few hours, but I'm afraid he didn't reveal anything new."

"So one of your detectives has already contacted the bartender at the Boutonniere to corroborate his story?"

"There's no need—everything he told us is lies. The guy in the cowboy hat, which is brown by the way, was an off-duty cop who called into the station first thing this morning when he heard the description of the person of interest go out over the police radio band. He told us our suspect was so drunk that he could barely hold his pool cue straight, which is why they only played one game."

"Then that's a lie and a truth."

"How so?"

"Your suspect told us he played one game, which was confirmed by the officer, and that he won, which was contradicted. So far not everything he told us is lies—only half of it…the trick is figuring out which half. I assume the officer told you there was no 'pertty' female stranger at the bar."

"It sounds like you're familiar with the Boutonniere…you ever seen any pretty female strangers in there."

"I met my Becca there."

"Yeah, but Becky's not a stranger."

"She was when I first met her."

"Well, she's not a stranger to most folks around here...and no, the officer reported it was just him, the bartender, our suspect, and a few other farmhands there—no ladies."

"Then the officer saw the suspect leave the bar?"

"No...he did say that when he left around eleven, the suspect was still at the bar—alone."

"Interesting," replied Weston. "Any chance I could get a look at his car?"

"You're really starting to sound like an actual investigator. Sure, they've got it locked up in the impound lot out back. You can take a peek through the windows, but obviously they don't want you touching anything inside."

****

Mayor McCormick walked Weston out to the coupe parked in the middle of the small, fenced-in lot.

"I was here when they towed it in this morning," said the mayor. "It's a real rust bucket...too bad he didn't take better care of it. I always liked these old Mustangs. I figure this GT must be an '89."

Weston peered through the passenger-side window. "No, it's more likely a '90...and it's not a GT."

"It's a V8...it's got the 5.0 badging right there next to your knee."

"Yes, I noticed that too, but this Mustang is a Fox body notchback, making it an LX not a GT. The third generation GTs were hatchbacks. Also, '5.0' is a misnomer. The V8 engines in this era of Mustangs had a displacement of 302 cubic inches or 4.9 liters. There's no reason to round up to a whole number when employing a decimal point."

"Okay, smart guy, but how do you know it's a '90 and not an '89?"

"The steering wheel is equipped with an airbag, which Ford introduced to the Mustang in the 1990 model year."

The mayor placed his hands on his hips. "What do you, like, restore pony cars in your spare time?"

"These days I spend most of my spare time changing diapers."

"Yours or somebody else's?"

"I'm not old enough and you're not young enough to be making that joke. In point of fact, I did some research into hotrods for *Speeding Spinster*. Did they pull any prints off these beer cans here?"

"Yeah, the techs dusted them and then put them back just as they found them. All the prints belonged to our suspect."

"That's curious."

"Why is that?"

"There wasn't a single print from anybody else? Your suspect must've gotten the beer from someone…who presumably handled it."

"Maybe he bought the beer at the bar, and the bartender's prints got washed away by the condensation on the cans."

"I'm fairly certain the Boutonniere only sells longneck bottles."

"Maybe nobody else handled them because he bought the beer at a liquor store and the clerk beeped the UPC with one of those laser deals."

"Under city ordinance, Mr. Mayor, all liquor stores are required to close at ten p.m., which is earlier than when the cowboy cop last saw him at the bar."

"So maybe he bought the beer first."

"And then went to a bar while it sat in his car getting warm—that doesn't make much sense." Weston studied the cramped backseat. "Did they happen to find the shotgun?"

"No, we didn't recover the weapon, only the spent shell from the crime scene. He probably tossed the gun into a cornfield somewhere afterward."

"There's not much inside the car other than the beer cans...anything interesting in the glove compartment or trunk?"

"A bunch of CDs in the glovebox—nothing at all in the trunk."

"Curious."

"You keep saying that."

Weston pointed at the driver-side window. "The CD player in the dash is an aftermarket Alpine...an expensive one back in its day—the kind typically used as a head unit for a system that includes a subwoofer, which is usually quite large and thus kept in the trunk."

"Perhaps he took it out and sold it for beer money."

"That could be, but then why not sell the whole system?"

"Because he's an idiot."

"That could also be."

"But you don't think so."

"That he's an idiot—without a doubt." Weston stood up straight. "That he shot Slim...I'm not so sure."

"What are you going to do now?"

"Drive over to the university to talk to a bunch of

other idiots and then maybe get a drink afterward."

Chapter 5

H.P. and Weston walked from the English Building to the nearby Design Building that housed the campus's diminutive modern art museum.

"I don't know why the university chose to have the presentation here," H.P. said. "For that matter, I still don't know why they decided to give me this award at all."

"As for why they chose to fete you among the modern art, they likely figured your gruesome mug would look more at home among a backdrop of abstract sculptures and paint splotches; as for why they decided to present you with an award…I honestly have no earthly idea."

"I appreciate you agreeing to introduce me. I feel as if all the professors in my department look down their noses at me because I don't have a Ph.D. and whatever flattering things they might say would be disingenuous at best, whereas you have a compulsion for speaking your mind and never give quarter to insincere flattery; however, I think it worth reminding you that this isn't a roast."

Weston opened the door to the museum for H.P. "Of course…don't worry, I'm confident you'll be pleased with what I intend to say."

"I'm not worried…just try not to piss anyone off— I do have to work with these people, you know.

Speaking of which, I should find the dean to let him know that we're here. You like cheesy stuff—go check out the Warhol hanging over there that we have on loan from the MoMA."

Weston did just that. He stood in front of the large soup can for a close inspection. A well-dressed woman with a glass of white wine sidled up next to him.

"Breathtaking, isn't it?" she asked. "We're lucky to have it—even for a short time."

"Yes, it was nice of Mama to lend it to us."

"Right…especially this one. As I'm sure you're aware, the gold banners on the label introducing the Cheddar Cheese variety makes this one unique in the series."

"Oh, I know. I have several of these at home myself."

"You have several Warhols in your private collection? I assume you mean his lithographs."

"No, I mean soup…in the cupboard—quite tasty on a cold day."

"I see…you were only japing."

"More joking, I would say." Weston scratched his head. "Though his brushstrokes are nothing to joke about—you can tell he painted this soup can with a soupcon of obsession."

"These were created using screen printing…a non-painterly process. You're not a very learned man, are you?"

"No, I am not, but I'd like to think I know a con job when I see one."

The dean took the dais and coughed into the microphone at the lectern. "Attention everyone, please find your seats, as we shall begin momentarily."

"Now if you'll excuse me, I have to go introduce the man of the hour in a few minutes."

After the turtlenecked men and pantsuited women took their chairs, the dean began his opening remarks.

"We have chosen to bestow our department's annual Nib Award on our guest of honor tonight both for his voluminous Pirate Hunter book series as well as for his fortitude in the face of this past year's tribulations involving a certain ex-faculty member whose name I'm sure we'd all like to forget. However, I'm sure you all feel as if you listen to me prattle on much too much in our department meetings as it is, so I've invited another prolific local author to introduce this year's Nib recipient. Without further ado, please give a warm welcome to the renowned romance writer, Weston Payley."

The dean returned to his seat as Weston took his turn at the lectern, adjusting the microphone as the clapping quickly petered out.

"Thanks for that lackadaisical round of applause and thank you, dean, for your introduction to my introduction. Now I've seen firsthand why your faculty meetings take twice as long as necessary. Speaking of introductions, it was lovely to meet you and your wife, Charity, during my last visit to campus, and with a face like yours her name would have to be Charity, wouldn't it? Incidentally, I wouldn't characterize my writing as part of the romance genre, but I digress—tonight's not about me...it's about my good friend H.P.

"As some of you may know, H.P. and I are coeval, though I think we can all agree that I look considerably younger. We've known each other a long time. Some years ago, when we were both but arrivistic young artists, we lived in the same dilapidated apartment building in the middle of Chicago. Our studio apartments were across the hall from one another, and on the weekends I'd hear the strangest sex noises coming from his room—mostly in the form of questions like, 'Where's my wallet?' and 'Doesn't my condition mean that I should only have to pay half price?'

"But the vicissitudes of a writer's career being what they are, things have changed since then—today he lives in a dilapidated farmhouse in the middle of nowhere, and now he is the recipient of the prestigious Nub Award...oh, I'm being told it's actually 'Nib' with an 'i'—like the point of a fountain pen. Okay...whatever. Anyway, when I agreed to this dog and pony show, I asked our guest of honor what one usually says at such an award ceremony, and to my surprise he told me he didn't know because he'd never won an award of any kind. I wasn't necessarily surprised by his admission, but rather that he'd stuck with writing for so long despite the lack of encouragement or any form of apparent praise. I mean you've got to admit, the guy's tenacious, and that has to count for something...or it should.

"However, as mediocre as his novels may be—which to me always read as if they were written by a middle schooler who writes at a nineteenth grade level—at least he has an imagination, unlike the rest of you automatons, who only publish to keep your silly jobs teaching nonsense to numskulls. I mean really, do you think anyone cares? Do you even care? A Marxist exegesis of *The Metamorphoses*...a feminist critique of James Fenimore Cooper? It's fine if you want to waste your lives with this bunkum, but when you tell students whose tuitions pay your salaries that this stuff is important, you're just stealing from them—not only their money but their time too.

"Though perhaps it isn't accurate to accuse you of being unimaginative. After all, it must take some amount of imagination to convince yourselves that you're royalty in the make-believe kingdom of academia rather than just irrelevant wonks in the real world. Half of you are overeducated morons and the other half boorish snobs, but what sticks in my craw the most are you sons of bitches right in the center of that Venn diagram.

"In closing, my friend doesn't deserve your department's award; he deserves a better department— one that values authors who make real contributions to our culture by writing things that people actually want to read."

Chapter 6

Weston and H.P. walked in silence to the Vivian Lee Memorial Parking Garage. As they entered the concrete structure, H.P. finally said, "Actually that didn't go as badly as I thought it might."

"Sorry if I got a little carried away...when I get in a room full of smarter-than-thou types it brings out my mean streak."

"No kidding—I thought the dean was going to cry."

"You must feel the same way, since you wrote how pompous all those professors are in that manuscript you had me look at before you sent it off to your publisher."

"True, but I was fairly confident that none of them were ever going to read it. Thanks to what you had to say tonight, I'm sure now they'll all read *Double Doppelganger* with great interest."

"So I helped you get some more book sales— you're welcome," said Weston. "Besides, like I told you before, you should be proud—it's a good story...just has a terrible title."

"Unfortunately, *Siamese Spinster* was already taken."

"Don't worry, we'll come up with a better title for our book."

"We should probably come up with a plot first."

"You're always by the numbers, aren't you?"

Weston stopped near his car. "Hey, let me see the pen they gave you."

"There's no pen."

"They don't even give you a pen for an award named after a pen part?"

"Nope, just a plaque to hang on the wall of my office."

"Plaque—I've got that hanging on the walls of my arteries, and all I did to earn it was eat too many cheeseburgers. Well, you're not likely to win any more awards in your lifetime, so let me buy you a drink to celebrate your new wall décor."

"Yeah, okay…though it'd probably be better if I— and certainly you—didn't show our faces this evening at my usual watering hole, the Faculty Lounge."

"That's fine…I know a place."

****

Weston parked his car in front of a cinderblock tavern.

"This is the place?" H.P. asked incredulously. "You've been here before?"

"They love me here." Weston stepped out onto the gravel parking lot. "It's a real high-class joint."

H.P. studied the blue and red neon sign overhead. "It reminds me of that roadhouse from *The Blues Brothers* movie."

"Great film—let's go inside and say howdy."

Weston and H.P. pushed through the double doors and took seats at the mostly empty bar. The bartender eyed the pair dubiously. "I remember you…you're that shit heel who told everybody this place used to be called the Boutonniere."

"I only told Slim."

"Well, somebody must've told everybody else then, because for about a month this place damn near turned into a gay bar, which would've been okay with me if the ones that came in here were city-slicker queers like you two, but we got all those rowdy backdoorwoodsmen—the kind who like to hang around rest stops late at night. I had to hire a few goons to run them off, because they were scaring away my regular customers. Smart asses still write 'Butt in Air' graffiti in the bathroom stalls, and don't get me started on the limericks."

"I'm surprised your restroom attendant stands for that," said Weston. "Barkeep, me and my thirsty friend would like two cans of your finest beer."

"No cans—just bottles."

"If it's all the same, I'd like something a little stronger," H.P. said. "A Scotch please, single malt if you have it."

"Trust me—they don't. We'll have two glasses of bourbon, preferably on the rocks, if you've had your ice machine fixed."

The bartender set up the glasses on the bar. "You're in luck. The repair guy got out of prison last month."

"And I'm sure our society is the better for it."

"I doubt it," replied the bartender, "but it beats drinking warm whiskey."

"Speaking of mischief makers who've had their scrapes with the law, I was talking to a fella earlier today that told me he was in here last night."

The bartender poured the whiskey. "Yeah, who might that be?"

"Instead of answering your question outright, since

he's not a regular and may not have formally introduced himself, let me tell you who he isn't: an off-duty cop or a farmhand."

"Last night, huh?"

"That's right—around eleven."

"Okay, I know the guy you're talking about…sort of a dipshit."

"That's as fair a description as any," said Weston. "He told me that he talked to a beautiful woman who bought him a beer, but then he has a proclivity for prevarication."

"I don't know about them last couple fancy words, but what he told you is half true."

"So what's the other half of the story?"

"You know, folks usually pay for answers to them types of questions."

"Would you perchance be interested in a prestigious Nib Award?" asked Weston.

"I don't know what that is, but I'm fairly sure I would not."

"I'm with you on that account," said H.P.

"How about the autographs of a couple of prominent writers that you could proudly display over your bar?"

"Who—like Tom Clancy and Stephen King?" asked the bartender.

"No," answered Weston. "I meant mine and my compatriot's signatures."

"I ain't got no interest in that, but you two are welcome to sign your names above the urinals."

H.P. pulled out his wallet and set a hundred-dollar bill on the bar. "I'm not sure why my friend cares so much about this aforementioned dipshit, but now my curiosity is piqued. He's buying the drinks, but allow me to leave the tip."

"You walk around with C-notes in your pocket?" asked Weston.

"Nobody but Romans call them that anymore," replied H.P. "I found myself short on cash last time I was in Chicago, so I tend to keep a little extra money on me these days."

"Are you some kind of secret millionaire? Do you have a million bucks?"

"I used to."

The bartender held up the bill to the light to inspect it for authenticity and then stuffed it into his shirt pocket. "So there was a gal in here last night for all of five minutes—a real looker too."

"Like a hooker looker?" Weston asked.

"Nah, I could tell from the way she talked she was high class."

Weston nodded. "So complete sentences—go on."

"Anyway, I guess she did technically buy dipshit a beer."

"Technically?" Weston shook his head. "How's that work?"

"She came in here and ordered a beer, I figure to pay for her spot at the bar; I never even saw her take a sip of it. She told me she'd been in here the other day and lost her cell phone, and I told her we didn't have any phones in our lost and found."

"Could someone have kept it rather than turning it in?" asked H.P.

"Could've I suppose, especially since we ain't got no lost and found, but it didn't matter…I knew the story was one of those—what'd you call it a minute ago…prevarications."

Weston tilted his head. "How'd you know she was lying?"

"Because I'm the only bartender that works here, and I damn sure would've remembered her if she'd been in before."

H.P. raised his hands expectantly. "So then what happened?"

"She was sure that she'd dropped it in the parking lot, but she couldn't remember exactly where she'd parked, and she didn't want to search the whole lot for a black phone in the dark, so she wanted to know if I had a surveillance camera set up out there."

Weston smiled. "But I bet you ain't got one of them either."

"Nope, I offered her a flashlight for her little snipe hunt, but she told me she'd come back and look for it in the daytime."

"Strange that she would come looking for it in the middle of the night at all." H.P. tugged at his earlobe. "I mean if she lost it the 'other day' you think she either would've returned sooner if she considered the missing phone so important or waited longer until daylight hours if she thought it so unimportant."

Weston folded his arms. "Now tell me about dipshit."

"Yeah, so he's trying to shoot pool with one of my regulars—the cop you mentioned—and making a real ass of himself, hitting the cue ball off the table, cursing up a storm. He stomps back to the bar after he loses and orders another beer. I told him he'd had enough, and so he sulks for a minute. I go down to the other end of the bar to get the farmhands another round, and the woman gives him her beer."

H.P. raised an eyebrow. "Then did they leave together?"

"No, she left right then. I reckon she felt bad for the dipshit and so offered him the beer she didn't want anyhow. I gave him the old stink eye, so he downed his beer and slinked out of here soon after."

"Any chance you still have the bottle?" Weston asked.

"Sure, I kept it as a souvenir in my treasure chest around back—looks just like a dumpster. Feel free to go rummage around for it. I can give you a pretty good description of the bottle…it's brown."

"And you haven't seen the woman since?" asked H.P.

"I mean she could've come back this morning before I opened…but, like I told you, her story was made up from the word go."

H.P. shrugged. "So why do you think she came in here?"

"I couldn't say for sure, but maybe she thought her husband was stepping out on her. She had a diamond ring on her ring finger that nobody who comes in here could afford…except maybe you two, you know, if you were into ladies. I figure that's why she asked about the surveillance camera—wanted to see if she recognized her husband's car on the video…maybe she suspects him of slumming with some cornpone hussy."

"That's not a bad theory," said Weston, "connects a lot of dots."

"Gee, thanks—that's high praise, coming from a romance novelist."

"See, I knew that you knew I was a writer."

****

The bartender set overturned stools on the bar next to Weston and H.P. "Okay boys, I hate to bring your date night to an end, but you can finish your drinks while I sweep up, and then you've got to go."

Weston nodded. "I hear you, barkeep."

"We've been sitting here for hours," H.P. said, "and we still haven't come up with a good idea of what to write about."

"I blame you for that. My original plan was to have your Pirate Hunter meet my Spinster in some alternate universe type scenario, but then a couple of weeks after you agree to collaborate on a book with me, you send me your latest manuscript that involves your Pirate Hunter in an alternate universe where he meets you."

"Sorry about that...I promise I'd been working on that story before you told me about your idea."

"I don't doubt it. No one could've come up with a manuscript that fast unless they'd experienced those events for themselves and merely transcribed all the details, and so far as I know you have not recently been transported to a parallel dimension, though there was that odd business with Fixer that you've never fully explained to me."

"Sorry again, but I was told by the authorities in no uncertain terms not to discuss the specifics of the case while their investigation is still in progress."

"But I'm a writer—I make stuff up for a living...who could I tell that would ever believe me anyway?"

H.P. finished off his whiskey. "Even if I told you the whole story, I think you'd likely find it too unbelievable for fiction."

"Be that as it may, I anticipate this latest manuscript of yours will be your biggest book ever—except, of course, for the one you've already agreed to coauthor with me. The story really breathed new life into your P.H. character...quite revelatory, though unfortunately now it makes him all wrong for a crossover—at least the one I originally had in mind. You know, I never think too highly of authors inserting themselves into their own stories—it's a hackneyed gimmick—but I really appreciated your approach. You didn't try to make yourself the protagonist or the antagonist...you were just a regular old agonist, stuck in between two versions of yourself, one of whom was your better and the other your worser, if you like."

"Yeah, I sort of portrayed myself as the middleman on the good guy/bad guy continuum...not quite suited to step into either role—an ineffectual, space-taker-upper."

"There's no reason to get down about it—I thought it rather inventive...or at least unique. Knowing me, if I'd gone that route, I probably would've cast myself as the unlikely hero—a fish out of water who somehow manages to save the day...possibly even written the damn thing in first person."

"Not even you are that big an asshole."

"I suppose if I was, I could always use a penname...maybe change the letters in my name around a bit."

"That's an easier code to crack when you've only got two letters in your name," said H.P. "Listen, tonight's been great...well, I guess that's not true, but the last hour or so hasn't been too bad, so let's not end the evening by stressing out over our story."

"Who's stressed? I'm reasonably confident that we'll eventually come up with a terrific idea. And if we don't, then we'll just slap something together anyway and chalk the whole thing up to a well-intentioned but failed creative experiment...then pay to get one of those Circus reviews for the back cover."

"You know it's pronounced Kirkus, right?"

"Oh, it's a hard 'C'?"

"No, it's a 'K'...both of them."

"What the hell is the point of the 'C' anyway? A soft 'C' sounds like an 'S,' and a hard 'C' sounds like a 'K,' so pardon the *kritisism*, but it seems to me that the 'C' is a *kompletely unnesessary* letter."

H.P. chose to ignore the half-drunken diatribe. "Also, Kirkus doesn't always write positive reviews."

"Now I know you're pulling my leg. Who in their right mind would ever pay for a negative review?"

"The thought of reviews for a book that hasn't yet been written is distressing...let's talk about something else. Has your daughter spoken her first word yet?"

"She's trying to say 'dada'...it comes out sounding more like 'mama,' but I know who she means."

"What you have is nice. You ever think about making the family official and marrying Becky?"

"Now you're distressing me," said Weston. "Do you remember when you turned fifty?"

"Sure, it was just last year."

"Then do you remember when you turned forty?"

"Yeah, I suppose."

"Did they feel any different?"

H.P. raised his head toward the ceiling. "Not really...fifty was like forty except my hair got lighter and everything else got heavier."

"That's how it felt for me too, until I met my Becca and had a kid with her. Now the stakes seem so high…add a marriage certificate to the mix, and I think I'd be that much more afraid of losing it all."

"I hear you my friend, but you can't live in fear. Does it feel right—your situation now…I mean down in your gut?"

"More than anything I've ever known, which makes me think it won't last…nothing good ever does."

"You could be correct, of course, but I've recently learned that sometimes it's better to trust your gut than your brain. Play the hunch—see where it leads…and that's the sum of the wisdom this middle-aged writer has gleaned over the years."

Weston considered the unsolicited advice for a moment as he finished his drink. "Barkeep, can I borrow your flashlight?"

"As long as you take it with you and don't bring it back tonight."

"What do you want a flashlight for?" asked H.P.

"To play a hunch."

****

Weston searched in the foliage along the periphery of the Boutonniere's parking lot as H.P. beat the bushes with a stick.

"So what are we doing out here?" asked H.P.

"Playing a hunch."

"You told me that part already, but I thought it meant you were going to go home and propose to Becky."

Weston swept the flashlight's beam from side to side. "Just keep looking."

"I don't think we have much chance of finding that

lady's mobile phone, and besides I doubt she would've lost it in the bushes."

"We're not looking for a phone."

The bartender rolled down the window of his pickup truck as he slowly pulled out of the parking lot. "Get a room you two. I don't want no funny business going down in my bushes. This here's a family establishment."

H.P. watched as the truck's taillights disappeared down the backroad. "He knows we're not actually homosexuals, right?"

"It is a small town, so it's hard to say for sure—anyone who doesn't chew tobacco and drive a vehicle capable of hauling lumber runs the risk of being thought a sissy."

"Comforting...so what are we looking for exactly?"

"You'll know if you find it."

"Care to be more specific? Like is it bigger or smaller than a breadbox?"

"It'll probably be about the same size."

H.P. whacked at another bush, and his stick hit something solid that resulted in a resonating sound, as if he'd beaten a drum. "I think I may have found it."

Weston walked over with the flashlight and shined it on the object discarded in the bushes. The light revealed an upholstered wooden box inset with a large speaker. "I'll be damned."

Chapter 7

Weston disrobed and slid into bed next to Becky, who was softly snoring. He tossed and turned a few times, but she remained asleep. Then he let out a heavy sigh, yet still she continued to sleep.

"Did you say something?" he asked aloud.

"What the hell…what time is it?"

"A little after midnight," answered Weston. "Did you ask me a question?"

"Yeah…'what time is it.' "

"Oh, I thought I heard you say something before that."

"No—I was sleeping."

"Well, now that you're awake, how about that radiator hose inspection?"

"Fellas who wake me up after midnight with whiskey breath and who skip medical procedures don't get their hoses inspected. The hospital called. What happened?"

"I was there…early even, but then I found out Slim was too. He got shot last night. I just called to check on his condition. The night nurse told me that he started to regain consciousness, but then they decided to put him into a medically induced coma to keep him from straining his heart. They still don't know if he'll make a full recovery."

"I heard he was in the hospital…you two have

gotten close this past year, haven't you?"

"He's the only redneck friend I have, and you know how important diversity is to me."

"How's his son?" she asked.

"He's staying with his mom now. The mayor told me he'd talk with him."

"That's good. How did the award thing go on campus?"

"Really terrible. I don't think anyone will ever ask me to do anything like that again, so I suppose that part worked out well."

"Did you and H.P. at least come up with a story for your book?"

"We discussed several ideas."

"Any of them promising?"

"All of his could best be described as either awful or dreadful."

Becky yawned and turned over. "I'm sure you two will think of something...now get some sleep."

"Okay, Becca." Weston rested his head on the pillow, but sleep would not visit him for some time.

Chapter 8

H.P. entered his darkened home. He snapped on a floor lamp, which minimally illuminated the living room. During these moments of entering his empty house in the middle of the night, he often lamented that his century old farmhouse had been constructed before homes were installed with electrical wiring in the ceilings for overhead lights. H.P. couldn't quite muster the energy to turn on the other two lamps in the room, so he sat down in his well-worn recliner and removed his mobile phone from his pocket. He considered the bright screen in the dim room for a moment before placing a call.

"Hello," answered a groggy voice. "What time is it?"

"A little after midnight, Vicky. Is it too late?"

"No…it's fine. How did the ceremony go tonight?"

"Weston was tremendous…said all the things I've wanted to say for years. I wish you could've been there."

"I know…I thought I could make it, but then they dumped this new assignment on me at the last minute."

"Sure, I understand. I watched your last segment on the evolution of the Me Too Movement."

"What'd you think?"

"I still say it's a silly name, but I thought the piece was poignant."

"Thanks." Vicky yawned. "I would've liked to have met Weston tonight…and, of course, seen you."

"It would've been nice to see you too. I can arrange an introduction next time you're in town."

"Are you two making any progress on that writing project of yours?"

"We bandied about a few ideas tonight, of which all of his were horrible. Did you ever get a chance to read that manuscript I sent?"

"I'm sorry…I've been so busy lately."

"No problem…I just thought you might find it amusing. I already emailed it to my publisher anyway, so probably better at this point to read the finished version when it comes out."

"I'll be the first preorder." Vicky waited a moment for H.P. to respond. "You sound down…tonight was supposed to be fun, no?"

"I'm just tired. You must be too, so I should let you get back to sleep."

"Okay, but I'll come visit you next time I'm in the Midwest."

"I'd like that. Maybe my publisher will send me on a book tour. I could stop by when I'm in New York."

"That'd be great, though it seems like I'm in L.A. more and more these days."

"I think they sell books out there too."

"Yeah, just nobody reads them."

"Goodnight, dear girl."

"Goodnight, old man."

Chapter 9

H.P. entered the classroom in the English Building where he taught his creative writing seminars and flicked on the fluorescent lights. Two rows of long tables faced each other. He took his usual seat at the head of one table in the spot farthest from the door. He preferred that seat so he could greet his students as they came in and see all of them at once when they each read their latest short stories or installments from their novellas in progress.

This was his 300-level seminar. Most of his students had taken previous courses in the program with him, which he considered a compliment, though there was usually at least one student who he wished would choose a different instructor. The one in this class was a lanky dunderhead who walked as if the floor under his feet was always slippery and uneven. This thin-faced aspirant fancied himself the next James Joyce and had mentioned a few too many times his intention to never work a real job, choosing instead to become a career novelist and not caring whether he ended up the successful or starving kind. *Talk to me in ten years,* H.P. thought.

As was his wont, this student was the first to arrive and took a seat next to H.P. at the head of the other long table, which irritated him—not because he minded sharing the front of the classroom, but because the young man's proximity meant that he had to turn in his seat to see him and alter the projection of his voice when he addressed him so as not to sound as if he were shouting. No other student ever sat in that seat; H.P. suspected the upstart wanted to be close at hand in case he ever felt the instruction needed bolstering.

"What's good?" The tall young man set his canvas messenger bag on the floor next to H.P.'s leather one.

"So many things," H.P. answered.

"That's what I like about you."

"Uhm...my inveterate optimism?"

"No, that you always say the same thing."

"You always ask me the same question."

"Yeah, we're a lot alike in that way."

H.P. returned to reading for the third time the short—nearly flash fiction—story in front of him that the class was scheduled to discuss. It was authored by a young woman who wrote succinctly, but whose stories, concise though they were, H.P. had never been able to follow. They all involved her, or at least a character very much like her as far as he could tell, trying to make what she considered to be a momentous decision; however, over the span of three separate classes in three different years, H.P. had never been able to determine what the decision was or even what it was about.

A few more students filed in as H.P. continued to pretend to be preoccupied, hoping to obviate the usual pre-class chitchat with his self-appointed teaching assistant. Finally, he looked up at the clock on the wall to see that it was one minute past the hour and took note that a quorum was present. "All right let's get started. Any thoughts or questions about process that have come up since we last met before we begin with our assigned story for today?"

The tall young man sitting right next to him raised his hand over his head. "I have a question." H.P. twisted in his seat to signal that he was listening. "As you all are aware, I've elected to write a novella this semester rather than three short stories…sure, it's a little more work but I think it's paying dividends, you know, as far as my craft is concerned."

"And what's your question?" asked H.P.

"Instead of calling it a novella, which sounds sort of negative, what if we all agree to call it a *yes-vella*?"

H.P. turned back to the others in the room. "Okay, I'd like to open that idea up to the class…thoughts?"

"I don't care," said a goth gal.

"I think it's cute," answered the featured writer for the day.

"It's maybe the dumbest things I've ever heard," said H.P.'s new favorite student.

"There you have it—a full spectrum of responses." H.P. turned once again to the young man. "Writing is all about making decisions, so the decision is ultimately yours, but be aware that there will be those who like what you have to say, those who don't, and still others who are indifferent."

"No offense," replied the young man, "but that's it…some people will like what you do, and some won't?"

H.P. wondered how much trouble he'd get into if he used his red pen to poke the tedious student in the eye. "That's not it…but that's certainly part of it."

The young man leaned forward. "Then what's the rest?"

"Well, as you've likely heard me say before, the

world is full of describers and experiencers, but if you want to be a good writer don't be either—be both…for the describers make mountains out of mole hills, and the experiencers have nothing interesting to say unless they've actually climbed the mountain; however, great writing exists somewhere in between."

The young man nodded. "Yeah, I have heard you say that before…like at least a couple of times every year."

"Then let us hope it sinks in. Now let's get started with today's story. Since the story is a little on the short side, I'd like to do something a bit different today and have the author give us a brief introduction before she reads it aloud."

"What do you want me to say?" asked the featured writer.

"Oh, whatever you feel like saying. Perhaps what you were thinking when you wrote it—what you want us to take away from it…maybe what it's about."

"It's about a relationship fraught with emotional turmoil."

"Fascinating," said H.P., "but if I'm not mistaken, there's just the one character in your story."

"The other characters are implied."

"I see. You know what, why don't we bag my introduction idea? Just go ahead and read it."

Chapter 10

His last class finished for the day, H.P. walked across campus to the Deluxe Bar, though the tiny hole-in-the-wall establishment was decidedly not deluxe in any way. He entered the narrow bar and took a seat on his regular stool.

"It's almost starting." The hoary bartender reached up to turn the dial on the antiquated television set.

"What's almost starting?" asked a fulsomely bearded man at the end of the bar, the only other patron in the place.

H.P. studied the bewhiskered man for a moment. "Edwin?"

"Oh, hey there H.P.—I didn't recognize you."

"Must be on account of the beard...wait, that's you. I haven't seen you in ages. What're you doing back on campus?"

"Just picking up some outmoded equipment that the astronomy department was going to throw away...and doing a bit of laundry."

"Are you still working on your cosmology theory out there in the woods at that old radio telescope?"

"Cosmogony theory, actually."

"What's the difference?" H.P. reconsidered his query. "You know what, I'm sure it's a long answer, and my show's about to start, so let me just buy you a beer instead."

"Fine by me. As I recall, you used to frequent the Faculty Lounge."

"Still do, but this place is closer to my office, so I like to stop in here from time to time."

The bartender set a cold beer in front of each of his patrons. "He comes in here most every day to watch that damn program of his. I figure he watches it here because if he went to a bar that actually had customers in the middle of the day, they'd all complain."

"I don't think it'd be the Faculty Lounge's cup of tea." H.P. took a swig of beer.

"So what's the show?" Edwin finished off the last of his old beer.

"Alternative World," H.P. answered with some discomfiture.

"The soap opera?"

"I prefer episodic melodrama…and I just bought you a beer, so don't ask to have it changed."

"I haven't seen any TV in months, so it's okay with me. Besides, this show's a classic—it's been on for decades. My mother used to watch it when I was a kid, but what's happening with it these days?"

"Well, the two main characters are still on it, though of course they're middle aged now. A lot of the supporting characters have changed, but some of the old ones still pop up occasionally. Last season the Wilton character moved to a small town and became embroiled in a mystery involving a nefarious pharmaceutical company that set up a clandestine operation in that selfsame town to covertly test a diabolical new drug. Meanwhile, the Hap character fell in love with a younger woman who left at the end of last season, but not before he had a mind-altering experience in which he believed he'd been transported to a parallel reality where he met different versions of himself—all played by the same actor, mind you. This season, he's dealing with the resultant heartache from the breakup as well as coming to terms with whether the whole other-dimensional event was just an elaborate dream or not. So now, after many years of independent plot lines, it looks as if the Wilton and Hap stories are going to intersect for reasons that hitherto have remained unrevealed."

Edwin furrowed his brow. "Wow, who writes that stuff?"

"Geniuses, my friend…pure and simple."

****

"I've got to say," Edwin said over the show's closing credits, "that was way more entertaining than I would've thought a soap opera—pardon me, an episodic melodrama—could be."

"I'm glad you enjoyed it," H.P. replied. "Let's have another round."

The bartender opened two more bottles and set the first in front of Edwin. "The show's a lot more entertaining when somebody else is buying the beer."

"Maybe you're on to something." Edwin gulped down the last of his old beer and handed it to the bartender. "Usually I drink alone and out of a jug, but still…I think the critics have these melodramas all wrong. I mean sure it's implausible, but who cares?"

H.P. nodded in agreement. "Precisely, as if plausibility is a writer's primary goal. If you're so hungry for plausible, then go to the damn grocery store."

Edwin grinned. "We still talking about the TV

show or has this turned into a literary discussion?"

"Speaking of literature, do you still have your collection of *Fantastic Four* comic books?"

Edwin took a long drink from his longneck bottle. "It's my only vice."

"If you ever want to part with the first hundred issues or so, I'd be willing to pay full cover price despite them being out of date."

"I'll keep it in mind."

"Hey, did you happen to know Weston moved out your way awhile back?"

"Yeah, he comes out to the telescope now and then...usually when he wants to pick my brain about something."

H.P. shook his head. "Sounds like Weston. The only thing that's changed about him since I knew him in Chicago is his hair color."

"He mentioned you two are collaborating on a book. He always tells people he doesn't write romance stories, and you tell people you don't write sci-fi adventure stories, so I'm curious what kind of story this one won't be?"

"At this point, I'd be satisfied with any kind of story that has a beginning, a middle, and an end...and I'm not even all that particular about the order."

"I take it the collaboration isn't going so well."

"I thought partnering up would be a good way to split the load, but so far it seems as if we're each waiting on the other to start doing the heavy lifting."

"Creative partnerships can be a challenge." Edwin finished his beer. "But I bet Weston will come through when it counts, though I wouldn't want to wager my Lee/Kirby comic collection on it."

"Maybe a jug of booze then?"

"Yeah, maybe that." Edwin stood and walked to the door, patting H.P. on the shoulder as he passed. "I should return to my telescope before it gets dark, but it was good seeing you—and you too barkeep."

"Take care, Edwin."

"See you next time," said the bartender as the door closed. "He's quite a character—that one."

"He must not come in too often. This is the first time I've seen him here."

"He stops by every couple of months—drinks one beer and then leaves…that is unless he can get somebody else to buy him more. It's strange, whenever I think to myself, *I haven't seen that fella with the beard in a while*, he's sure to turn up the next day or so."

"That is strange. Well, I should go too. I've got some work to do before dinner."

"Your usual reservation?"

"The food's lousy, but I enjoy the company."

Chapter 11

H.P. returned to his little office in the basement of the English Building where a big stack of students' stories awaited him atop his desk. Just as he settled in and started to read the first one, the dean knocked on his door.

"Sorry to bother you so late in the day, but I've got a quick question for you." The dean took a seat.

If it's so quick, then why sit down? "Sure thing, and by the by, my apologies for Weston's comments last night. He has a unique sense of humor. He's very self-defecating."

"I think you mean self-deprecating."

"No, I mean he frequently shits himself...like a lot."

The dean's face turned red as he snickered. "Yes, I wish that he'd appreciated the gravitas of the proceedings a bit more, but we stodgy academics understand how off the cuff and from the hip you creative types sometimes speak. However, that's not why I stopped by. As you may recall, I asked you last year if you wouldn't mind taking a meal from time to time in the dining hall of the dormitory over on the next block."

"Yes, I remember. I stop in about once a week. I was planning to have dinner there tonight, in fact."

"Very good then. I asked the same favor of all the

staff members in our department, but it has come to my attention that almost none of them honored my request."

"Well, a lot of the others have families that they want to get home to. I don't and, as it also happens, I'm a terrible cook; as such I've unintentionally trained myself to better stomach the dorm food, which anyone with functioning taste buds would find disagreeable."

"I appreciate you being such a good sport about it. Originally, that's why the chancellor had asked us deans to make the request of our respective department members to occasionally visit the dorm dining hall nearest to our buildings—sort of a show by the university that the much maligned dorm food must not be so bad after all if we feed it to our professors and such, though as far as can be determined, it's done nothing to change the low opinion of the offerings of the campus cafeterias."

"Perhaps the chancellor could consider the inferior dorm food to either be motivation for our philistine engineering students to seek out the finer things in life after landing lucrative jobs post-graduation or preparation for our epicurean humanities students to be content with eating from trash cans as they struggle to find employment after graduating."

"I'll be sure not to share that thought with her when next we meet." The dean's face grew serious. "However, there are new concerns of late on the cafeteria front beyond the usual complaints about the quality of the food."

"What are those?"

"Unfortunately, there has been something of an uptick in the number of students admitted to the infirmary who have succumbed to the temptation of illicit drugs, which resulted in what I am to understand were highly realistic and intricate hallucinations. As you are no doubt aware, recreational drugs are no stranger to our campus; however, what's unique about several of these cases is that upon being interviewed by the campus police after their recovery from these hallucinatory episodes, the students in question claimed that they did not knowingly ingest any mind-altering substances. Of course, the police initially believed that the students were merely attempting to evade disciplinary action, but further investigation revealed that this latest group of students all reside in the same dormitory, which compelled the administration to look more closely at the infirmary data, and it was discovered that over the past year every time there has been a spike in such cases, most of the students were part of the same residence hall cohort."

H.P. thought several thoughts at once as he pulled on his earlobe. "So the campus cops think the dorm food is being dosed?"

"No, they don't think that exactly, or otherwise the university would shut down all the dining halls and incur a sizeable pizza bill. However, the chancellor thought it worth having the deans ask the faculty if they'd noticed anything out of the ordinary."

"When you say 'anything out of the ordinary' you mean drugs, right? The stench of marijuana on some of the students is quite potent, but it's also quite commonplace and so by definition not out of the ordinary...in addition to being nearly legal. Besides, if cafeteria workers were lacing the food with enough marijuana to cause the kind of hallucinations you described, it wouldn't go unnoticed by anyone. They'd need garbage bags of the stuff to spike a whole meal service, which would be one expensive practical joke."

"Well, I—or rather the chancellor—thought it worth asking. Please do let me know if you happen to observe anything odd or improper."

H.P. nodded. "I will...of course, you're welcome to join me for dinner tonight. I think pasta is on the menu. The students refer to it as fettucine I'm-afraid-of."

"Thank you for the invitation. Regrettably, Charity and I are expecting guests for dinner this evening, but bon appétit."

Chapter 12

Waiting in line to get into the dining hall with students who were less than half his age made H.P. feel much more than twice as old but also gave him a sense of connection, reminding him that he was part of a larger community rather than a small inner circle. Besides, delaying the time until he would actually be eating the cafeteria food was no great sacrifice. When it was his turn, he presented his faculty ID to the student checking meal-plan vouchers at the door. The young woman inspected his ID and gave him a look as if to ask, *Are you sure about this?*

H.P. continued on in the line, first taking a tray and then two plates and flatware. When he finally arrived at the long buffet, he eyed all the options: a deep pan of thick noodles, a large vat of cream sauce, a big plastic basket of bread, a wide platter of iceberg lettuce, and, of course, the ever-present trough of Jell-O…the flavor of the gelatin du jour—yellow. H.P. took some of everything, loading up both plates. At the drink station, he poured himself a mug of coffee, a glass of milk, and a cup of juice.

He walked with his conspicuously laden tray to a small, empty table and sat down. Sometimes former students would sit with him and sometimes he would eat alone, but even when he sat by himself, he never felt quite as lonely as he did when eating at home in front of the television.

"Whoa, that's a lot of food," said a plump young man who H.P. vaguely recognized. "You carb-loading for a marathon or something?"

"I doubt I could drive twenty-six miles without getting winded. Feel free to join me, if you like."

"Sure." The student set his tray on the table. "You may not remember me. I signed up for your intro to creative writing class last year, but I dropped after a couple of weeks. It wasn't anything personal; it was just too early."

"My own creative juices don't start flowing until well after lunch." H.P. noticed that the young man's plate was mounded high with fettucine noodles covered in red sauce. "I only saw the alfredo. I didn't realize there was also a marinara option."

"There wasn't. This is my own recipe: one-part Italian dressing and two-parts ketchup."

"How very ingenious."

"Yeah, the grub here's not great, so sometimes you have to get inventive, though it looks like you don't mind the food. I can't remember ever seeing anybody actually taking the Jell-O."

"I thought I'd try some of everything tonight. Do you have a favorite food here?"

"I like the chicken fingers. I once ate fifty of them." The young man beamed with pride.

"As part of some sort of *Cool Hand Luke* themed contest?"

"Is that a movie or something?"

"They made a book out of it too. I understand the dorm food isn't too popular, but is there one dish in particular that students detest the most?"

"The meatloaf is pretty infamous. They always serve it a day or two after Salisbury steak. We figure they must grind up the leftovers we send back to the kitchen and then bake them in loaves."

"Could be."

The young man became distracted by a group that sat down two tables away. "Oh, those are some of my online gaming buddies. Do you mind if I—"

"Not at all," interrupted H.P. "Game on."

"Thanks." The young man stood with his tray. "It was nice talking with you. Maybe I'll sign up for your class again next semester."

"I'll be there."

The young man left the small, quiet table for the larger, louder one. H.P. returned his attention to the food on his tray. He'd planted the seed of marijuana in the dean's head to distract from the more obvious possibility that the dorm food was being laced with lysergic acid diethylamide. Thanks to Weston, H.P. now had concerns that people in his department might actually read his forthcoming novel, which in places could seem like an account of an acid trip. Between the antagonist being loosely based on a former member of the department and the description of an affair with another faculty member, he was worried that some might think he'd started self-medicating in order to draw inspiration from his real life. H.P. wanted to put as much distance as possible between himself and the notion that he was creating fiction from one-part reality and two-parts special ketchup. Of course, the thought had occurred to him that the events of his latest manuscript had been the result of being surreptitiously dosed with a mind-altering substance, perhaps by some disgruntled chem student who'd concocted a batch of LSD or something like it in a campus laboratory to exact revenge for receiving an unfavorable grade in one of his creative writing courses, which were often and erroneously perceived by science majors as being an easy A. However, until now it hadn't crossed his mind that he might not have been specifically targeted.

The Jell-O suspension made the most sense as a vehicle for the drug, but the portly student had told him that hardly anyone ever ate it. A liquid drug could be added to anything of course, but likely it would lose some of its efficacy if heated, so that partially ruled out hot food like the noodles or sauce. Certainly it could be sprayed on lettuce or bread, but due to the potential for runoff with the lettuce and uneven absorption by the bread, the application would be inconsistent, and it seemed unlikely to H.P. that someone with the fastidiousness to create the drug would be satisfied with it being applied so haphazardly. *Whoever's doing this— if someone is in fact doing this—would want the maximum result for their efforts.* H.P. turned his attention to the drinks. Again, coffee probably wouldn't be the best choice since it's hot, and the milk would be difficult to tamper with, as the sealed plastic pouches it came in were only opened when installed into the dispenser. That left the juice, which was made from a concentrate...*easy enough to mix in an extra ingredient.*

H.P. set the small cup of juice aside and took several thank you bites and sips of everything else, sniffing his food and stirring his drinks while he chewed and swallowed, looking for what he didn't know. Having eaten about a third of the food on his tray and thinking both that he'd had enough so as not to feel as if he was wasting it but also like he couldn't stomach any more, he took his coffee thermos from his messenger bag, dumped its remaining contents into the half empty coffee mug on his tray, and then poured the juice into the thermos. He left his table, placing his tray on the conveyor belt that disappeared back into the kitchen. As he exited the dining hall, he wondered if his leftover noodles would find their way into some future casserole.

Chapter 13

The next morning, H.P. arrived on campus early, stopping by the neurobiology department before he went to his office. He knocked on the dean's door.

"Come," a curt woman's voice commanded.

"Hello." H.P. tentatively opened the door to the spacious and very modern office—a far cry from his or even his dean's office in their department's antediluvian building. "I teach creative writing over at the English Building."

The stern-looking lady behind the desk studied him for a moment. "I suppose that makes more sense than teaching creative writing at the Applied Sciences Building."

"Yes…I suppose it does."

"So what can I do for you?"

"I was wondering if you might assay a sample I have with me for…hallucinatory properties." H.P. pulled the thermos from his bag.

"If you want a urine analysis, I suggest you go to the medical center. This may come as a surprise to you, but brain scientists are very squeamish about bodily fluids."

"No, it's just juice—a colleague was concerned that one of his students might've slipped something into his drink."

"A colleague, huh? I can have one of my grad

students take a look later today to see if the sample contains any foreign particulates, but as far as determining if those particulates have 'hallucinatory properties'…well, that would be rather tricky—unless you give me twenty bucks, in which case I'll make one of them ingest the sample."

"I appreciate you helping a relative stranger, but having just met you, I've got to say, it's hard to tell if you're joking or not."

"It's my delivery, isn't it? I'm too straitlaced. My improv coach warned me about this."

"You take improv classes?"

"That was also a joke. Just leave the sample on the edge of my desk there."

H.P. looked at his thermos. "Oh…I assumed you'd want me to pour it into a beaker or something. I have a full morning of classes to teach, so I was going to stop by the union to fill my thermos with coffee to help me through to lunch."

"Let me make sure I understand. You intend to use the container you brought the liquid your 'colleague' is concerned was dosed with a hallucinogen…to drink from?"

"I was going to rinse it out first. You should read some of the stories that I have to critique this morning…on second thought, you probably shouldn't."

The dean rummaged around in a drawer and produced a coffee mug that read *World's Grooviest Brain*, placing it on the corner of her desk. "You can pour it in there."

H.P. carefully transferred the apple juice from his thermos into the mug as she eyed the golden liquid skeptically. "I promise, it's not piss."

Chapter 14

H.P. made it through his morning classes, but several students had scheduled appointments to stop by during his afternoon office hours.

The first appointment belonged to an eager student with an outsized imagination. "Here's the idea for my next story: the protagonist has a multicultural background and can call upon the aptitudes of all his ancestors, such as channeling the cardiovascular capabilities of a Kenyan or an Inuit's ability to withstand extreme cold. The antagonist is the opposite; he has an unalloyed bloodline, but he has access to all his ancestors' memories and shares their innate desire to rule."

"To rule?" H.P. tilted his head sideways. "Like the world?"

"Yeah, for starters."

"Well, that sounds ambitious…both for your villain and for you, since the next assignment is to write a short story—like five pages—about family."

"But this is all about family. I see my bad guy as a pale Nordic type, and the hero as a swarthy-skinned pirate sort, but maybe toward the end they find out that they're actually related."

"Toward the end of your five-page story?"

****

H.P. flipped through several pages stapled together.

"I'd like to discuss your last story."

"Pretty good, right?" replied the supercilious student.

"There were some good things in it to be sure, but then there's also always room for improvement."

"Should I have used a different font or something?"

"No, the font's fine, but let me ask you...what were you trying to convey with your two characters?"

"You see, the first character is a very tall man who speaks slowly, and the other character is a homunculus who speaks very quickly. I tend to write a lot of dialogue, like you."

"Right, that's a good description of the characters themselves, but I'm more curious about the meaning of the dialogue you mention as it's comprised entirely of random song lyrics that don't appear to have anything to do with the rest of the story."

The student smiled smugly. "At first glance."

"Well, I glanced at it several times and still failed to discern any relevance."

"A homunculus is a very small human."

"Yes, I know what a homunculus is."

****

"Do you mind if I share my opening with you?" asked the coquettish student. "You know, the first couple lines of the story I'm working on now. I can read them to you if you like."

"Sure, that'll be fine," answered H.P.

"I tend to write a lot of dialogue, like you, so it starts with two people having a conversation. 'The legs were firm and the breasts plump, but the thighs were the most succulent part of all. Wait, she replied, are you talking about the turkey or the stuffing?' "

"Those…are the first couple of lines?"

"Yeah, I think I'm going to entitle this one: The Intern Gives the President a Tour of Her Oval Orifice. It's a double entendre."

"I believe that may only qualify as a single entendre."

"I also use a lot of wordplay in my writing the way you do. Want to hear this funny joke that I'm thinking of including in my story? Though I should warn you, it's a little naughty."

H.P. shook his head. "I don't particularly care for off-color humor."

"Why do penises have holes in them? Because men need open minds."

"I get it, so back to your story—"

"I'm sorry, but I've always wanted to ask you…what does the 'H' in H.P. stands for? It's not by chance Humbert, is it? That was the name of my last boyfriend."

"You don't really need to come see me anymore during my office hours. You're a capable writer; we can just discuss your work in class—that'll be fine."

"But I like to get your opinion of my writing performance…you know, one on one."

H.P. wished she hadn't closed his door so that people out in the hallway could see in or, if it became necessary, he could quickly escape from his office. "Well, you can always call if you have any questions."

"Great, can I have your home number?"

"No, I meant call me here…at my office—during the day."

"Sure…is it okay if I email you too?"

"Of course…though it might be best if you also did so during the day."

****

H.P.'s office phone rang. He lifted his head off the desk to answer it. "Yes."

"This is the dean over at the neurobiology department. We talked this morning."

"Was that just this morning? It seems like ages ago."

"Yeah, you sound tired. Anywho, you can tell your colleague that no one's trying to poison him. The sample you brought in is just apple juice, though of a markedly low quality."

"Thanks, I'm sure he'll be relieved hear that. If my colleague happens to come into contact with any more suspicious foodstuffs—"

"You can bring them by, though it's too bad…until recently we had a preeminent behavioral neuroscientist doing a fellowship with us who was aces at identifying those sorts of chemicals, but sadly the brain researcher left us due to a broken heart."

****

H.P. gathered up the papers on his desk that he hadn't gotten to yet and carefully crammed them into his messenger bag. He slung the bag over his shoulder, pushed in his chair, and flicked off the light switch near the door. Then the phone rang. He stared into the dark office for a moment and then turned the overhead light back on.

H.P. picked up the phone. "Hello."

"You sound tired, old boy," replied Weston.

"That seems to be the prevailing opinion."

"Want to get a drink?"

"All we do is drink. We should be writing."

"So is that a no?"

"No," H.P. answered.

"It's a yes then?"

"Yes, but I'm not going back to that roadhouse where the bartender thought we were a couple. I'm not offended that he thought I was gay mind you, but rather that he thought I couldn't do any better than you."

"Yeah, that bar can be a little uncouth, but I know a nice place called the Shady Tree."

"Sounds pleasant enough."

Chapter 15

Weston and H.P. pulled into the crowded parking lot of the Shady Tree. Weston parked his car in a spot between two Escalades.

"There sure are a lot of Cadillacs here," H.P. observed.

"It's a real high-class joint." Weston opened the driver-side door, careful not to ding the door of the vehicle next to his.

"That's what you said about the last place."

"Well then, eventually I'm bound to be right."

As the two entered the dimly lit tavern, every head seemed to swivel in their direction.

"We sort of stand out," H.P. whispered. "Are you sure we're welcome in here?"

"They love me here."

"You said that about the last place too."

Weston and H.P. took seats at the bar. The bartender looked them up and down.

"Two Canadian whiskies on the rocks, please," Weston ordered. "And yes, I'm sure we're in the right place."

When the bartender left H.P. turned to Weston. "Maybe the reason bartenders tend to think we're on a date is because you keep ordering my drinks for me."

"Trust me, I'm saving you time."

"So is this a bar for a biker gang? There were

several motorcycles parked near the entrance, and I noticed that the jackets many of the patrons are wearing have the same patches on them."

"Yeah, they're called the Ebony Enforcers—most of them are guards of the security and prison variety."

"And how do we fit in?"

"We don't, but one of their members helped me out with a case awhile back, and I think I might need her help again."

"Like a 'case' of wine?" H.P. squinted at Weston. "You're a romance writer...since when do you solve cases?"

"I don't really see myself as a romance writer."

"So you told my dean two days ago."

"As it happens, not all the stories I write are completely fictitious."

"I suppose there might be more of that going on than the general reading public realizes."

The bartender returned with a bottle, set two rocks glasses on the bar, filled them both with ice, and then poured the whisky.

"Thanks, my good man." Weston handed the bartender a twenty-dollar bill. "I came here looking for a pretty lady."

The bartender pocketed the twenty, giving no indication that he intended to make change. "You and just about every other dude in here."

"This happens to be a particular lady...with an afro and an attitude."

"You'll have to be way more specific."

"I think I know who he's looking for." A woman approached the bar who fit the description. "Hey Weston, what brings you back here?"

Weston smiled. "I was hoping we could chat. Can I buy you a drink?"

"You'd better not. I'm on a date, and he's the jealous, weight-lifter type."

"Things didn't work out with you and Geoff?"

"He was fun for a while, but then he got all clingy."

"That's too bad." Weston pointed to H.P. "Permit me to introduce another, less parasitic friend of mine."

"I know you...you're the author of that Pirate Hunter series, aren't you?"

"Yes, that's right," H.P. answered proudly.

"I really enjoy those books, man...I've read 'em all."

Weston raised his glass. "You must be very well read then, having read all of his Pirate Hunter books and all of my Spinster books."

"No, I only read the one of yours."

"Ah...well that's not important now." Weston put his glass down. "A friend of mine was shot three nights back, and now he's in a coma."

"Yeah, I heard about Slim...I'm sorry."

"I realize you're with a different department, but I was wondering if anyone has been talking...chatter on the police grapevine so to speak."

"Not really. I mean every time something like this happens, all the cops talk about it, but there haven't been many details. Why are you asking, anyway?"

"I had a chance to interview the suspect they have in custody, and I don't like him for it."

" 'Like him for it'...I think maybe you've been watching too many *Law & Order* reruns."

"You might be right, but still something seems off.

71

The perp has a criminal record, but no history of violence. However, aside from my initial interview, I'm getting zero cooperation from Slim's department."

"That could be because you keep saying things such as 'perp' and 'like him for it.' Listen, I know he's your friend, but he's their friend too, and they're not going to stop until they get a conviction…you know, beyond a reasonable doubt. No offense, but they probably don't want some wannabe detective interfering with their investigation."

"I think there's something bigger going on here." Weston shook his head solemnly. "Something the local police just aren't equipped to handle."

"And you are?" She arched her eyebrows. "The romance writer."

"I don't think of myself so much as a romance—"

"Man, I don't care if you think of yourself as Ian Fleming. This is the real world where sometimes some son of a bitch goes off crazier than usual and does stupid shit that don't fit his damn modus operandi!"

Weston nodded. "Point taken, but the only thing I can't do right now is nothing."

"I get it…you want to help your friend, but you'd be more help to Slim if you're there waiting with him when he wakes up. I'll tell you what, though—I know Becky…unfortunately, I send a lot of clients her way. If I hear something that I think might be of interest to you—that I also think won't get you into any trouble—I'll pass it along. Okay?"

"Okay…thanks."

"No problem, but now I should get back to my date before that vein in his neck pops. It was nice meeting you, H.P."

"Lovely meeting you as well."

"I can hardly wait to read your next book." She waved goodbye.

"That's quite a lady." H.P. waved back. "Terrific taste in literature too."

"Shut up."

"I saw on the news about that officer who was shot, but I didn't realize you knew him. If there's anything I can do to help, let me know. I understand how difficult it can be to just wait around. It's important to keep your mind occupied so as not to go mad from worry."

"Thanks…I guess I could use someone to bounce a few ideas off of."

"I can be bouncy—springy that is, not bubbly."

"Of course, I doubt you'll be able to make any direct contribution to my investigation, but perhaps you'll unwittingly say something that I barely pay attention to, which will ultimately spark a thought that allows me to ascertain the machinations that I suspect are afoot."

"That would only work if I was your sidekick," said H.P. "If anything, you'd be my sidekick."

"But it's my case."

"It's not your case. Like the lady just told you, it's the police's case. You are acting as if you're an expert in writing procedural crime narratives; you write stories about an unmarried woman with an improbable number of avocations. You know, the character I write actually catches bad guys…like all the time. Besides, which of us has the more sidekick sounding name, Watson—sorry, I meant to say Weston."

"Fine, you won't be my sidekick per se…more like a partner—after all, not every partnership is fifty/fifty."

"That's for sure." H.P. took a drink. "You've hardly done half the work in our writing partnership."

"I've come up with my share of ideas. You're just too myopic to appreciate them. What's your latest idea that's so great?"

"I don't know…how about something involving a homunculus?"

"What the hell is a homunculus?"

"A miniature person…I had to look it up."

Chapter 16

She'd been living out of a suitcase for weeks now, moving from motel to motel in and around the same small town that she was sick of the moment she arrived. She returned to her room after her morning run and finished off her exercise regimen with some calisthenics. Then she showered and dressed before her daily call at ten o'clock.

She always wore professional clothes for her video calls—she'd learned the importance of structure and routine in the military—though of late, she'd started substituting flipflops for heels. Sitting at the desk in front of her open laptop, she put on her headset and keyed in the access code to join the meeting with her handler.

"How are you today?" the digitized voice asked as a profile picture appeared on her computer screen. She figured the headshot was likely an image pulled randomly off the internet that bore no actual resemblance to her contact. Perhaps one day she'd be shopping for a sweater as a Christmas gift on the J. Crew website and see the same man with the cleft chin, wearing a cable knit pullover.

"I'm fine, though anxious to complete this assignment and move on."

Silence—the encryption lag made these calls feel interminable. "What is the police officer's condition?"

"He's still in a coma. If you'd authorized me to take a headshot, instead of being concerned about the hit looking too professional, he'd be in the ground now. I can pay him a visit and finish the job if you like. There's only one sentry posted at the door, and the cop on the night watch usually dozes off around midnight."

Quiet…she wondered if the idea was being mulled over. If her contact had to check with a superior, she could be waiting for a response until lunchtime. *Maybe I'll go back to that Mexican restaurant where I had those delicious enchiladas earlier in the week.* "Negative. The action against the police officer was only meant to rattle the cage of your primary target."

"Why rattle his cage rather than simply putting him down?"

She studied the eyes of the sweater model as she waited for a response. *Maybe I could try to look him up after this assignment is over and see if he has a girlfriend.* "The client wants to squeeze the primary before snuffing him. Your next target is one Edwin Hubert. I'm emailing you his details now. He resides in the area, though his exact whereabouts are unknown."

"If he's around here, I'll track him down. It's a small town—someone knows where he sleeps. Is this a kill order?"

She knew the answer before she asked the question, but it was always best to doublecheck about such matters. She hoped they wouldn't assign her the same subcontractor as they did last time; he talked too much. She felt as if she had to wait in that Mustang's cramped trunk forever while he nattered on with the cop before finally uttering the go phrase. "Just as before, extermination of the target is permitted but not

76

required. You'll be paired again with the same support operative. Move on target tonight if possible. The client wants to make a statement—the unequivocal kind."

I believe an explosion qualifies as unequivocal. "Copy that. I'll need to take the day to prep if I'm to be active this evening, which means I don't have time to waste finding a new motel today, even though it's my scheduled relocation day, so can we change the time for our call tomorrow? Either earlier or later is fine, but check out time at this dump is ten, and I can't check into a new motel until at least noon, so unless you want me to report the details of the operation from my rental car in a parking lot with who knows who walking past or from a stall in a public restroom, we'll need to move it."

She slipped on her diamond ring as she waited for a response. It made her feel better to wear something so expensive in a place so cheap.

Chapter 17

Weston waited in a hallway of the hospital in an uncomfortable chair, made all the more uncomfortable by a uniformed police officer hovering a few feet away in front of the door to Slim's room.

"If you want to go get a cup of coffee, I can watch the door," Weston said to the young officer.

"No thank you, sir."

"Son, you don't have to call me sir."

"I do if you call me 'son'...reminds me of my father, an ex-marine, who I always called sir."

"You sure you don't want to grab a sandwich or something?"

"I cannot abandon my post, sir."

Weston shook his head. "I'm not talking about abandonment; I'm talking about lunch."

"I will be relieved by a fellow officer at my designated mealtime."

"Okay, have it your way—just makes me feel anxious to be so close to someone standing at attention all the time. Can I at least get you a chair?"

"No thank you, sir."

"All right, let me know if you change your mind."

"Would you please stop bothering the officer?" Mayor McCormick approached with two cups of coffee.

"I was just trying to be nice." Weston reached up

for one of the cups.

"It's not for you." The mayor handed a coffee to the young officer.

"Thank you, sir."

Weston watched as the officer took a sip, and then he turned back to the mayor. "What about the other one?"

"I already drank from it. I'd have brought a third, but I've only got the two hands."

"I don't understand why they won't let us wait in the room with Slim." Weston shifted in his chair. "What are they worried about...that we're going to wake him up?"

The mayor sipped his coffee. "Only family is allowed in there, and aside from his boy, he doesn't have any."

"That's a brilliant policy...remind a patient how alone he is by not letting visitors into his recovery room."

"They'll let us in once he regains consciousness—until then we'll wait."

"The officer here is being paid to wait, and I'm a writer, which means most days I have nothing better to do with my time anyway, but don't you have a town to run?"

"It'll keep. People know where to reach me if there's an emergency. Over the years, I've clocked a lot of hours waiting in this hospital."

"For your son?"

"Yeah, him...and others. Patience is like any other skill; it takes practice to get good at it."

Weston leaned back in his chair. "I hope I never get that much practice."

"You've been here all morning. Why don't you take a break? If he comes to, I'll be sure to tell him how long you've been waiting."

"I suppose a temporary change of scenery might be good for my sanity."

Chapter 18

During the course of her current assignment, she'd spent many an evening patronizing dive bars—as if there were any other kind in the area—in order to study the local yokels. Now, thanks to her latest intel, she found herself at a comic book shop in the middle of the day and discovered what the two establishments have in common—they're both populated by idiots.

"Can I help you, miss?" asked the clerk behind the counter.

"Maybe. I'm looking for a birthday gift for my fiancé."

"What's he like?"

"Cleft chin...dreamy eyes."

"No, I meant what does he like...what's he collect?"

"Oh, right...*Fantastic Four* comic books. He's a fanatic for the whole quartet."

"Okay, so is he more into silver age or bronze age comics?"

"Was there a golden age?"

"There was," the clerk answered, "but the *Fantastic Four* wasn't a part of it."

"As you can probably tell, I don't know much about any of this stuff...what's the priciest issue?"

"Well, that would be issue number one that came out in 1961."

"Great, I'll take a copy, please."

"We don't have anything like that here. I doubt even Bonaparte Comics over by campus would have that."

"Shoot." She stomped her foot. "Is there any place around here that would? I'd be glad to pay top dollar. I'm kind of in a bind as my fiancé's birthday is tomorrow, and the surprise trip I'd planned just fell through because the pilot of the plane I chartered came down with the flu. Trust me, you don't want to be stuck on one of those tiny little jets with someone who's sneezy."

The clerk eyed her diamond ring. "Yeah, I believe you. I know a local collector who could have a first issue that he might be willing to part with for the right price."

"Wonderful, would you be so kind as to give me his phone number?"

"If he had one, I would. You see, he's a bit of an eccentric."

"Perhaps his address then?"

"I guess he's really more of a hermit than an eccentric. He lives out in the boonies…in an old, run-down radio telescope."

She shook her head. "Ah, a hard man to find."

"Yeah, you'd have to take a lot of unpaved backroads to get there. I could try to give you directions, but—"

"I'm not sure it's a good idea for me to go traipsing into the woods alone, looking for a complete stranger. It'd be better if I had a guide who could make the introductions."

"I get off in a few hours. I could go with you to

help you find the place. If he is willing to sell, I could also authenticate the comic book and make sure you're getting a fair price...you know, for a finder's fee."

"That sounds reasonable."

Chapter 19

While he was in the midst of a disquisition about some damn thing, H.P. saw Weston peek his head inside the classroom door. "Oh boy."

" 'Oh joy,' is right." Weston stepped into the room. "I imagine your students would welcome a visit from a real-life, working writer."

"What are you doing here?" asked H.P.

"I looked for you in your office, but a nice lady told me that I could find you in here."

"What lady?"

"A nice one."

"I recognize you," said a young woman, "aren't you Weston Payley...the author of *Scholarly Spinster*?"

"Indeed I am. That's one of my earliest books, back when I thought higher education was the key to intellect, not the unlockable door I know it to be today."

"Oh boy," H.P. repeated.

"I'm picking up what you're putting down, dude," said a militant young man.

"I'm glad to hear it," Weston replied. "And what sorts of stories do you write?"

"Dude, I write stories so dangerous that my words have to be sprayed with mace and birth control."

The young woman rolled her eyes. "His last story was about a bad break up."

"That bitch did me wrong, and now she gone."

"Gone all the way back to her last boyfriend, is what I heard," said the young woman, "a hockey player."

"Dude can have her for all I care."

"If you care so little, then why'd you write a story about her?" she asked.

"For your information, in case you can't remember all the way back to last week, my story was about how I'm better off without her—H.P., isn't that how you interpreted it, dude?"

"Oh boy."

****

The class concluded, H.P. and Weston walked toward his office. "Gosh, that was fun. I do so enjoy your little visits to campus."

"I thought a delightful conversation was had by all," said Weston.

"It was verbose, I'll give you that—so much so that we didn't get to the Tim O'Brien short story I had assigned."

"They can carry the thing over until next week."

"So why exactly are you here?"

"To invite you to dinner tonight," answered Weston. "Then maybe afterward we can do some brainstorming."

"That sounds like a lovely evening. I'll bring a bottle of wine."

"Bring two—a red and a white—I have no idea what we're having."

Chapter 20

Weston and Lance were playing a racing video game in the living room when Becky and Vance came through the front door.

Becky set a heavy bag on the couch. "You're supposed to be helping him with his math homework."

"My day was fine, Becca," replied Weston, not taking his eyes off the screen. "Thanks for asking...how was yours?"

"Busy, then I had to pick this one up from his 4-H outing on the other side of town, now I have to see about dinner, and then I suspect I'll need to help Lance with his homework."

"A woman's work is never—"

"Don't give me the 'woman's work' thing...I'm not in the mood."

Lance looked up at his mom. "You seem like you're in a mood."

"Nice one," said Weston.

Becky huffed into the kitchen as Van took off his coat.

"How was the service event?" asked Weston. "And before you reply, just tell me first which of the two categories what you're about to say falls into: complaining or bitching. That way I'll be prepared with the appropriate response: 'uh oh' or 'oh no.' "

"I was working like a straight up B-A-L-E-R,"

spelled Van.

"I think you forgot an 'L' there," Lance said.

"Nah, little man, I didn't," replied Van. "They had us baling hay. How is baling hay supposed to help me get into college? Don't you go to college so you don't have to do things like bale hay?"

"All your bellyaching makes me want to buy a set of those noise-canceling headphones and then strangle you with the cord." Weston turned away from the screen to look at Van. "4-H will look good on your college application...raising your GPA would look even better."

"Woohoo." Lance raised his hands in victory. "I just won. That's three races in a row...you slow old man."

"Call me slow or old again, and I'm going to donate you to an orphanage."

"Stop threatening to donate my son to an orphanage," Becky shouted from the kitchen. "My sister will be here soon with Ance, and I think she's going to stay for dinner. Frozen pizzas sound okay?"

"Sure, though maybe put in an extra one. I forgot to mention that H.P. is stopping by for dinner too."

Becky emerged from the kitchen with a chef's knife in her hand and a sour expression on her face.

Weston looked up at her. "I'm not the gourmet that you are, but I wouldn't start slicing the pizza until after it comes out of the oven."

****

H.P. sat next to Becky's sister Kim at the dining room table. "This pasta is delicious."

"Thanks," Becky replied. "It's just something I whipped up."

"You're not kidding." Weston twirled a mound of spaghetti around his fork. "She literally microwaved the sauce right before you got here."

Becky shot him a look.

"Ouch," Weston exclaimed, "someone accidentally kicked me under the table. I meant it as compliment to your ingenuity…besides, I was the one who opened the jar, so we all made our contributions."

"I would've prepared something a bit more elaborate had Weston told me ahead of time that you'd be joining us this evening."

"Sorry to be a surprise," said H.P.

Becky smiled. "A very pleasant surprise."

"While these noodles may not have required much preparation, I assure you that they're far superior to the last pasta dinner I had."

"Eating at the dorm again?" asked Weston.

"I'm afraid so." H.P. shook his head. "It must be difficult to cook with love when you measure ingredients by the gallon."

Kim set down her wineglass. "Becky mentioned that you two are collaborating on a book. So speaking of cooking, what sort of heat level are you anticipating between the Pirate Hunter and the Spinster?"

"I'm afraid that so far it's somewhere between tepid and room temperature," answered H.P.

"We're having a bit of trouble coming up with ideas that we both agree on." Weston took a drink of wine. "It might be a case of too many chefs in the kitchen, but we'll work through it."

"Or kill each other trying," added H.P.

"Maybe your characters could kill each other off instead," suggested Lance.

H.P. dabbed some sauce at the corner of his mouth with his napkin. "Oh, I hadn't thought of that angle."

Weston nodded. "*Slaughtering Spinster* does have a nice ring to it."

"That sounds like the worst idea since sliced dead," said Van.

H.P. chuckled. "I think we just found our tagline."

"It's surprising that you two haven't accomplished more in all the time you've spent working together." Becky sipped her wine. "Incidentally, a deputy stopped by my office today with a juvenile addict who she thought could benefit from an emergency session. She also happened to mention that she saw you both last night at the Shady Tree. Perhaps spending so much time at bars is part of the reason you haven't managed to make more progress with your writing project."

"I was there asking if she knew anything about Slim," Weston said.

"Isn't that a job for the cops?" asked Kim.

"They think they already have the right guy."

Becky put down her wineglass. "Which means you think they have the wrong guy."

"Which means I'm not convinced, so I'd like to find out for sure."

H.P. turned to Weston. "Has your friend's condition improved any?"

"His anesthesiologist has started to slowly lower his level of sedation, so he'll likely regain consciousness in the next couple of days. Once that happens, they'll know more."

"I'm hoping for the best." H.P. poured himself some more wine. "And how about the young addict...were you able to help him?"

"Maybe," said Becky. "It's so hard to tell. Some leave my office saying they'll never touch drugs again and then get arrested for possession the next day. Others are like talking to a brick wall, but sometimes something resonates, and they turn their life around."

H.P. reached across the table to fill Becky's glass as well. "I have no doubt that being a drug counselor is as challenging a job as it is an important one."

Becky sighed. "Thanks...yeah, it's made all the more challenging by the everchanging variety of drugs these kids are being exposed to—from meth, to opioids, to now something called seed corn."

Weston frowned. "What the hell is that?"

"It's so new that we're not even sure yet," Becky answered. "All we know is that it can cause temporary psychosis resulting in elaborate hallucinations."

H.P. returned the wine bottle to the middle of the table. "That's interesting...concerns have been raised recently on campus about a drug fitting that very description."

"That doesn't surprise me. So far, the users we've encountered are mostly in their late teens and early twenties."

"Did the deputy instruct you to tell me about this seed corn?" Weston asked.

"No," answered Becky, "she only mentioned that she saw you. She didn't 'instruct' me to 'tell' you anything."

"So then she didn't instruct you not to tell me either."

Becky stared at Weston. "What are you even talking about? Are you on drugs right now?"

Chapter 21

Weston and H.P. drove down a desolate, dirt road. Weston decelerated when the beams of his headlights reflected off a pair of taillights ahead.

"You promised Becky we weren't going to a bar tonight," said H.P.

"That's right, I did."

"So where are we headed on this dark road?"

"We're going to talk to a guy who knows about chemistry…and other things."

"A guy out in the middle of the woods who knows about chemistry…does he cook meth?"

"No, he's a friend of mine—smart as they come. His name's Edwin Hubert."

"Oh, you're taking me out to his telescope. I've always been rather curious about that."

"I didn't realize you two were acquaintances."

"I've seen him around campus over the years…we have similar tastes in television programs."

"Is that a fact?" Weston brought his car to a stop behind a late-model sedan parked in front of a "KEEP OUT" sign suspended across the narrow road by a rusty chain. "It seems Edwin knows more people than I was aware of…I've never seen another car out here before."

"If he has company, maybe we shouldn't bother him."

"He probably already knows we're here from my

headlights. It'd be rude to drive off without saying hello."

"If you say so."

Weston opened his door. "Is that a rental car sticker on the bumper?"

"I believe it is."

"Let me out," someone shouted from inside the trunk.

The two hurriedly approached the sedan.

"Are you okay?" Weston asked loudly.

"No," answered the person within, "I'm locked in a trunk."

Weston turned to H.P. "How do you suppose he got himself stuck in there?"

"Can you find the release?" H.P. asked the trunk's occupant. "Most newer cars have one—probably looks like a small cable."

Weston gave H.P. a quizzical look. "How do you know that?"

"Research for a book…the Pirate Hunter was locked in the trunk of a car driven off a pier."

"I can't reach it. My hands are duct taped behind my back."

"I'd better go check on Edwin." Weston took off in a run, hurdling the chain stretched across the road.

"I'll stay here and see about getting this fellow out, but yell if you need me."

Weston ran into the woods toward the massive telescope in the clearing beyond the trees. As he entered the clearing, he heard screeching tires off in the distance. Weston threw open the door to the telescope's housing and found Edwin duct taped to a chair near the control panel. He pulled the strip of tape from Edwin's mouth.

"Get out of here," said Edwin. "There's a bomb."

"Where?

"I don't know. I was unconscious when they planted it, but they left in a hurry, so you'd better go too."

Weston scanned the interior of the immense telescope; there were wires and jerry-rigged electronic contraptions everywhere as well as about a thousand different nooks and niches among the bulkheads in which to hide a bomb. Weston took out his pocketknife, a souvenir from a certain rangemaster, and cut away at the tape restraining Edwin. Finally, he sliced through enough of it that he was able to pull Edwin free. They both ran out the door, through the clearing, and into the woods.

Believing they had reached a safe distance and feeling protected among the trunks of the sturdy trees, they turned and looked at the telescope with anticipation—then waited…and waited.

Eventually, Edwin said, "I'd have thought the bomb would've gone off by now."

"Maybe it was a dud."

"All my research is in there…I think I'll quickly go retrieve—"

The telescope suddenly exploded in an enormous fireball that lit up the night sky and hurtled bits of metal in every direction, many of the pieces striking the trees around where Edwin and Weston would have been standing if not for the concussive force from the blast that knocked them both to the ground.

Chapter 22

Red and blue lights from police cars, firetrucks, and ambulances reflected off the gray smoke that permeated the woods. Mayor McCormick surveyed the scene of the recently extinguished conflagration as the county sheriff gave him the rundown.

"The firefighters were able to confine the blaze to the clearing," she said. "Had it reached the trees, where we're standing now would be engulfed in flames, and the fire likely would've spread for miles in every direction."

"That's good news," said the mayor.

"Now for the bad. I had a deputy call the rental car agency about the sedan we just towed away. It was rented online several weeks ago at the airport near campus using a corporate credit card. We'll drill down some more, but so far it looks like the card was registered to a dummy corporation. We didn't find anything useful in the car…no receipts or personal effects. We'll dust for prints, of course, but…"

"It'll probably be a dead end too. How's everybody doing?"

"The store clerk who was trapped in the trunk is still a bit shook up. His theory is that this was all an attempted heist of some very valuable comic books—go figure. He was able to give a decent description of the driver—apparently she was attractive…and I

94

believe he used the word 'sophisticated.' "

The mayor nodded. "That is right up until she stuffed him into the trunk."

"No, we think she had a confederate follow them out here as the clerk gave her directions. He was knocked unconscious from behind as soon as he got out of the car while she was still inside. Likely her partner parked a little ways off, came through the woods, and bushwhacked him. The EMTs say he probably has a mild concussion."

"What about Weston and Edwin?"

"Multiple lacerations each, luckily none of them severe. Edwin also has a concussion, so as a precaution—given the cuts and his knock to the noggin—they had a wagon transport him to the hospital for observation after we questioned him. He got a good look at a male perpetrator but not the woman—seems they grappled as she snuck up behind him and then hit him over the head. One bright spot in all this for him is that he keeps his aforementioned comic book collection at a secure storage facility and not on the premises."

"And how about the other one?"

"H.P. sliced his writing hand trying to pry open the trunk lid, so the EMTs bandaged him up, but otherwise he's fine."

"How do you know it was his writing hand?"

"Because I asked him for an autograph," said the sheriff. "I have one of his Pirate Hunter books in the glovebox of my patrol car. It's a good read."

"Jesus, another writer. I miss the days when this area was only populated by illiterate hicks. Well, since we're outside the township's limits, this obviously falls under your jurisdiction, but let me know if my officers can do anything to assist."

"Will do." The sheriff left to check on her deputies.

Mayor McCormick walked over to H.P. and Weston, who stood near his car. "How you boys doing?"

"Aside from my backside being peppered with shrapnel and a ringing in my ears that still hasn't abated, I'm peachy," Weston answered. "H.P., let me introduce you to the town's mayor."

"Nice to meet you. I'd shake your hand, but it's bandaged at the moment."

"So I heard," said the mayor.

"Did you also happen to hear if there are any leads?" Weston asked.

"The sheriff told me her team is following up on a few things, but nothing promising yet."

"Are they looking at a connection between Edwin and Slim?"

"Should they be? I didn't realize they knew each other."

Weston shook his head. "I don't think they do, but that doesn't mean their situations aren't connected."

"Doesn't it? They don't know each other, and the circumstances are completely different—one was shot, and the other had his house, or whatever you want to call it, blown to bits."

"I'm the connection. They both knew me."

"No offense, but so what? I'm the mayor of a small town, which means I know almost everybody, and when misfortune befalls two of my friends, I don't automatically assume it's part of some conspiracy with me at its center. I know you writers like to put yourselves in the middle of everything, but sometimes shit just happens that has nothing to do with you."

Weston folded his arms. "Can you at least tell the sheriff to look into the possibility of a connection?"

"Does it look like we're in town? I can't 'tell' her to do anything. She informed me of the situation out here as a courtesy, but this is a county matter. However, every law enforcement officer in these parts is aware of Slim's situation; I assure you he's at the forefront of their thoughts, so if during their investigation anything pops up linking this incident to that one, you can bet they'll be on it like stink on a skunk."

Chapter 23

Weston gingerly repositioned himself as he drove H.P. back to his car at Becky's house. He shifted his weight from here to there, but no matter how he sat it hurt. "I think I'm going to have to start writing while standing up like Hemingway did."

"He was plagued by severe hemorrhoids," H.P. said, "whereas you just have minor cuts."

"They're both a pain in the ass."

"That reminds me, how did your colonoscopy go?"

"It got sidetracked by Slim's shooting."

"You're the one who really shot him, aren't you? Shame on you...all to get out of a routine procedure. You know, it's important for guys our age to get our insides checked out."

"Sure, but it's easier for you since you're able to perform the exam yourself—what with having your head up your ass most of the time. So what do you think?"

"Meh, not bad...but not great. I wouldn't include it in a book or anything."

"As if I would ever be so desperate for material that I'd write about a conversation with you," said Weston. "No, I meant do you think there's a link between what happened to Slim and Edwin, or do I have my head up my ass too?"

"It's hard to know for sure, which I guess is why

it's called a mystery. From what you told me about your chat with the dipshit—and given the fact that he was so drunk he could barely play pool—it seems unlikely that he's the shooter. And the comic book clerk's theory that the explosion back there was the result of a robbery gone wrong doesn't hold any water. You don't try to rob a bank and then blow it up if there isn't any money in the vault. However, it's easy to connect those two dots when you can only see the pair of them."

"Maybe, though I think the cops are a little too eager to make their own connections."

"Possibly, but like the mayor told us, you seem pretty eager to make your connections too."

"So you think the cops are right?"

"I don't know if they are or aren't, but in my research over the years, I've come to understand that law enforcement officers—just like the rest of us—are susceptible to confirmation bias. If they can make charges stick to someone that's already in custody and who's a known menace, it's often a better proposition than chasing after someone else who could prove too elusive to catch...a bird in the hand and all that."

Weston looked over at H.P. "What do you think about the term *seed corn*?"

"It means start-up money for a business enterprise."

"Right, that makes me think this new drug is just the beginning of something big. Slim's attempted murder a few nights back led us to the deputy last night, which in turn led us to Edwin's attempted murder tonight. So now I suppose—connected or not—we have to figure out where it all leads next."

"See, you're doing that thing where you leave out parts of the story to create a more streamlined and plausible narrative. The deputy didn't lead us anywhere with the phrase seed corn; Becky just happened to mention it. And talking to the deputy last night didn't actually yield any illuminating results, just like coming out here tonight to talk with Edwin probably wouldn't have shed any light either. They were both just shots in the dark."

"A friend once told me that sometimes you have to take a shot into a dark cave and then wait to see what runs out."

"Sounds like a really good way to get mauled by a bear."

Chapter 24

Having her check-in call at eight o'clock rather than ten had thrown off her morning routine. She hadn't had a chance to exercise and so felt like she was sitting on pent-up energy in want of an outlet, though that feeling may have also been partly the lingering effect of last night's explosion. Blowing stuff up always caused her to have an acute visceral reaction.

The J. Crew model appeared on her laptop's screen as the electronic voice asked, "How are you today?"

"Fine thanks, though I'm not looking forward to checking into yet another dumpy motel this afternoon."

She'd considered more than once during her years of working for the association of simply staying put in one motel rather than moving every three days as was the protocol, or maybe even flouting altogether the regulation requiring associates on assignment to stay in low-budget lodgings that likely had lax security and asked few questions of their guests. *It's not as if my handler would be able to tell the difference from what little of the room he or she could see behind me on our calls.* Though she figured the association likely tracked her laptop's location.

"I think you'll be glad to hear that the client has decided to initiate the final stage of your assignment."

"That's good news. I take it the client was pleased with my work last night."

She usually traveled someplace warm after an assignment—*a couple of weeks in Belize might be nice*. Then she would often visit her mother in Omaha or her sister in Seattle for a few days. After that, she returned to her apartment in Montreal to await her next assignment.

"On the contrary, they were quite displeased. The client wanted to make a statement but characterized your latest action as reaching the level of a full-throated proclamation. However, I was able to appease them by pointing out the subjectivity of their instructions as well as underscoring our superlative track record with their organization. So now they want to bring this campaign to a conclusion."

"Okay, how do they want it done?"

Ugh, grow a spine already. She figured the client was probably some sub-rosa subcommittee whose members had worked themselves up into a frenzy about this romance writer for whatever reason, but now that things were actually happening, they'd developed misgivings. *It's easy to talk tough in a boardroom, but when you see the results of your words on the news…it can change your perspective.*

"Put some of the individuals you've been grooming into play. Make it messy but utilize the research you've done in the area to give this the appearance of a localized event—nothing too grand in scope…no more explosions. I'm emailing you Weston Payley's address as well as some other pertinent details now. Obviously, the client doesn't want his extermination traceable in any way back to them, or us for that matter."

"Copy that."

As if the Keystone cops around here would even be

capable of comprehending a picture that big. She knew just the hayseeds to pin this on. After all the nights spent drinking bad beer in seedy bars, listening to their endless hunting stories—as if killing something incapable of shooting back was remotely impressive—not to mention the flirting, debasing herself by pretending that the filth who pawed at her could ever be in her league...finally, it would all pay off and she'd get her payback as well as a substantial paycheck.

"Once again, you'll be paired with the same operative."

"I think the guys I have in mind will be plenty. I don't need a support operative. What I need is a new car...wait, no, a truck—a big one."

Chapter 25

Having spent much of the night tossing and turning, mostly sleeping on his side, which he was unaccustomed to, Weston awoke in the morning with more aches and pains than usual. He slowly put on his robe and tentatively descended the staircase.

"You doing okay, pin cushion?" Becky poured him some coffee as he entered the kitchen.

"I didn't realize I'd slept in so late."

"You had a big night." She handed him the coffee mug and kissed his cheek. "It's been all over the news this morning. Almost makes me wish I hadn't made you promise not to go out to another bar last night."

"Despite feeling like I sat on a cactus, I'm glad I was there to help Edwin. Any mention of him on the news?"

"Only that a local astronomer is listed in fair condition at the hospital."

"Good. I thought I'd go over there this morning to check on Slim and then pick up Ed. I'll let him bunk at my place, since I hardly ever stay there anymore. Do you need me to drop off any of the kids?"

"Nope, already taken care of."

"I thought the house seemed unusually quiet."

"Speaking of houses, I've been meaning to ask why you're still hanging on to your granddad's old place…as you just mentioned, you've hardly been there in months."

"That's because thus far I've been lucky." Weston set the coffee mug on the counter and pulled Becky in close. "I figure sooner or later you'll wise up and throw me out...then I'll need a place to stay."

"I don't see that happening. In fact, I took the morning off, so we could spend a little time together— just the two of us."

"Two-of-us time...that's been in short supply of late."

"Well, we could keep talking about it in the kitchen or go back up to the bedroom and do something about it."

"You'll have to take it easy on me. I'm a wounded man."

"Don't worry, I'll be as gentle as an angel."

"That'll be a change of pace."

They left the kitchen and began climbing the stairs—her eagerly and him slowly.

Becky looked down at Weston from the top step. "Are you coming or not, old man?"

Weston rubbed a hamstring. "You know, we almost never fool around on the living room couch anymore."

Chapter 26

After reviewing the information her association handler had emailed, she closed her laptop and opened her flip phone.

On the second ring, a gruff voice answered, "New Dawn Munitions and Survivalist Emporium—we carry an extensive line of magazines for both your arms and your mind."

What absolute morons. "Hello, is Matthew there?"

"Who?" asked the voice pointedly.

For pity's sake. "The Sergeant at Arms—is he available?"

"He's back in the stockroom, hang on." The gruff voice yelled, "Matt, you got a call—I think it's a female."

I'm surprised this troglodyte knows the difference.

"Yellow, this is Matt. What can I do you for?"

He's as witty at work as he is at the bar. "Oh, Matthew, you say such clever things."

"Jade, is that you? I haven't talked to you in a while. I didn't know you knew where I worked."

You only mention it every time I see you. "Sorry to bother you at work sweety, but—"

"It's no bother at all. I'm trying out a new shipment of crossbows that we just got in."

Those'll come in handy next time you need to repel a siege of a medieval castle. "Fascinating, listen my cousin told me that big government ATF agent I mentioned was asking questions in town about the local gun shops—sounds like he aims to shut them down and collect information about their customers."

"Not while I'm still breathing, and we still have a Second Amendment."

I'm surprised he can count that high. "Well, my cousin knows where he's staying—a quiet house out in the country, so we're planning to go over there today and talk some sense into him. Want to come with us, sugar?"

"Hell yes, I do."

"Great, we'll swing by your store later to pick you up."

"It's actually an emporium," said Matt.

"Copy that."

"So what should I wear?"

The same mismatched camouflage ensemble you wear every time I see you will be fine. "What do you mean, honey?"

"You know, should I wear a bulletproof vest or night-vision goggles…something like that?"

"I think a simple ski mask will do."

"I don't ski, but how about a bandana over my face."

"Sure, see you soon, sweetheart." *And then if all goes well, never again.*

Chapter 27

Weston knocked on the door to Edwin's room and entered. It was a welcome change to be allowed admittance to the recovery room of a friend.

"You look like hell," Weston said.

"And you look surprisingly chipper. You took as much shrapnel as I did. Why do you seem to be in such an uncharacteristically good mood?"

"It's a good day…one friend is scheduled to be discharged today and another is anticipated to come out of his coma tomorrow."

"I'm pleased Slim is expected to regain consciousness soon. I've heard you speak very highly of him on several occasions."

Weston swiped at the air. "Ah, the guy's just okay."

"That's high praise, coming from you."

"The nurse at the front desk told me that the doctor wants to take one more look at you before she lets you go, but then we can get out of here. Since you're between places, you're welcome to stay at my house, unless you'd rather I drive you to campus to see Kate."

"Oh, she's not exactly in the picture any more…her fellowship is finished."

"That's too bad."

"The longer she's away, the more I'm inclined to agree with that sentiment."

"You did almost get yourself killed last night...you could call her. I'm sure she'd be glad to know that you're doing all right."

"Perhaps I'll send her an email when I get a chance."

Weston shook his head. "Very romantic...don't forget to add some emoticons to really spice things up."

"Being a romance writer doesn't automatically qualify you as a couple's counselor. In fact, it might disqualify you."

"Maybe so."

"With all the excitement last night, I didn't get a chance to ask what brought you out for a visit."

"I'm not sure really...just to see how you were, I guess."

"I don't think you've ever once stopped by when you didn't have a question about something."

"In the light of day it sounds a little ridiculous to say out loud, but ever since that business with Big Pharm that I consulted with you about awhile back, I keep thinking I see bogeymen lurking in the shadows."

"Just because saying it sounds ridiculous, doesn't mean they aren't there."

Chapter 28

After her initial success of securing local firepower for the evening's operation, she'd struck out twice to enlist homegrown muscle. Just as he was about to agree to come with her, the girlfriend of the country hoss from Cattle Tipper's Saloon got on the line and told her never to call again or she'd chop off her head and puke down her neck—*not very ladylike...and who can vomit on demand*? Then the steroid addict she'd met at Pump's Juice and Whiskey Bar cried into the phone for half an hour about his pet ball python that was missing, presumably having slithered away from home.

She perused the few contacts in her burner phone. *Hopefully the third time will be the charm, or else I'll actually end up needing the services of that same stupid subcontractor the association insists on having tag along.* She made a call.

"Sons of Uncle Sam Motorcycle Club—live free and never stop riding. If you're calling about our Pro-Freedom Road Rally this weekend, it's been canceled due to the threat of inclement weather."

Is there such a thing as an anti-freedom rally? "Hello, I'm calling for Brent."

"Sure, just a sec...I think brother Brent is throwing darts."

She had trouble picturing a man with hands as big as his throwing anything smaller than bowling balls.

"Yo, this be Brent."

How can a man that large have a brain that tiny?
"Hey Brent baby, do you know who this is?"

"Olive—that you?"

"You betcha, dearest."

"I ain't seen you around lately."

"Been busy babe, but I thought you might be interested to know my cousin told me that commie-fascist agitator is back in town trying to stir up trouble again…says he's going to overthrow the government."

"Not on my watch he's not."

"I thought you might feel that way. My cousin knows where he's staying—a quiet house out in the country, so we're planning to stop by later today. Want to come along?"

"He ain't like your kissin' cousin, is he?"

"No dear, we're just the regular, non-making-out type cousins."

"That's good to know. I don't want to get mixed up in one of those situations again."

I have got to get out of this backwoods burg. "So darling, are you interested in coming with us to talk some sense into this rabble-rouser?"

"Sure, sounds like fun…what should I wear?"

Oh, for crying out loud.

Chapter 29

Having no classes for the day, H.P. sat at the writing desk in his well-lit attic. He thought perhaps his and Weston's strategy of coming up with the plot for their manuscript first was in error. Maybe they'd do better to each take turns writing installments. If he wrote the first chapter and then handed it off, perhaps Weston could expand on the story in ways that hadn't occurred to him and vice versa. It seemed like a sensible plan, but so far his morning's efforts had resulted in a short scene of the Pirate Hunter and the Spinster sitting in a café, having a brief discussion that in no way advanced the narrative.

Frustrated, H.P. closed his laptop and pulled out a legal pad and pen. Lately he'd found that writing in longhand often helped to get things going, but as he put pen to paper his bandaged hand objected with a sharp pain. He returned the pad and pen to their drawer and opened his laptop again, clicking the dictation icon in the toolbar of the document he'd been working in.

H.P. cleared his throat. "The Spinster and the Pirate Hunter continued to drink their coffee in the café."

He read the words on the screen aloud. " 'The sphincter and the irate nutter continued to brink their golf fee in the calf eh.' "

He pondered the sentence for a moment. "At least it's original." The words, *At least it's original*, appeared on the screen. He shut his laptop once more.

H.P. leaned back in his desk chair and stared at the attic's cracked window. Not wanting to clean the windowpane too vigorously for fear that the glass would crack further or break altogether, the window had developed a thick film during his residence at the old farmhouse that only made it useful for letting in ambient light rather than actually seeing outside, though it still served to indicate the approximate time of day. The penetrating rays of the midmorning sun shone through even the opaquest of smudges on the glass, filling the room with a radiance that invited wistful thinking.

H.P. thought about the character he'd known for so many years, having only published some of the Pirate Hunter's stories, choosing to keep others just between the two of them. With the room so quiet, he could still hear echoes of last night's explosion. *Had the Pirate Hunter been there, somehow he would've been at the center of the action rather than on the periphery attempting to liberate a goofball from a car trunk.* H.P. wondered if things had worked out better with P.H.'s Victoria than they had with his. He missed the Pirate Hunter. These days the window to his world was frequently more difficult to see through than the one he was looking at now.

H.P. stood up from his chair and stretched his arms out wide. Then he crossed the room to the filing cabinet where he kept his half-baked ideas and quarter-completed projects, some of them dating all the way back to when he'd been a college student. *Revisiting a piece I previously put aside could prove useful, since all I'm trying to do is get the story started...that's not self-*

plagiarism, right?

He opened the top drawer and randomly pulled out a set of pages stapled together. He began to read, turned the first page, and then cringed. He tossed the paper to the floor. *That one shouldn't have been visited in the first place, let alone revisited.*

H.P. continued to sift through pages in the drawers, occasionally finding what he considered to be a gem among the dreck. After a couple of hours spent reading, he'd managed to pile a short stack of pages atop the filing cabinet that he felt contained some viable possibilities. He looked at his watch; it was later than he realized. H.P. grabbed the stack of papers and headed for the stairs, careful not to slip on the numerous pages littering the floor. He'd agreed to meet Weston that afternoon at his house to discuss their story in earnest, away from the distractions of a noisy bar or noisy children or noisy college students—a nice conversation at a quiet house out in the country.

Chapter 30

She watched from the window of her second-floor motel room as a crew-cab pickup pulled into the parking lot below.

There's my ride. She grabbed her go bag and exited the shabby room for what she hoped would be the last time. She descended the stairs as the association's mandated subcontractor rolled down the truck's window. "Give me the keys. I'm driving."

He reluctantly got out of the driver's seat and tossed her the keys. "The association wanted me to pick up the pickup—figured a little lady renting such a big truck might make an impression on the clerk at the rental counter."

"Makes sense—now get in the back."

"The product from the client is in the center console." He opened the rear door of the crew cab.

"Good...no, the way back. I need you to ride in the bed."

"How come?"

"Because the two guys I'm picking up each think the other is my cousin. If there's a third guy, it'll just be confusing for them, and we need these village idiots for this operation to look like a local job."

"Yeah, but the association wanted me to come along to keep an eye on you—make sure you don't blow anything else up or otherwise get carried away."

"Fine, but this is a three-person operation—any more than that, and we'll be bumping into each other. I'm the op-leader, and I'm telling you that you're the odd man out, so get in the bed of the truck. Take a nap if you want…this'll most likely be the easiest assignment you've ever had."

"But the truck's got this hard-shell tunnel cover." He knocked on the protective lid covering the bed.

"Right, it's a rental—they don't want you scratching up the bed of their truck moving your grandmother's piano…climb in through the tailgate. And incidentally, the word is 'tonneau'—it's French."

"But it doesn't unlock from the inside."

"Neither did the tiny trunk of that jalopy I had to hide in the other night—just hold it closed like I did. At least you'll have more room to stretch out."

He pulled down the tailgate and examined the short space between the floor of the bed and the ceiling of the tonneau cover. "I don't think this is best use of my talents."

"You're not understanding how important your role is in this operation. I'll be working with two untrained buffoons. If at any point something goes sideways, I'll shout: I need something from the truck. Then you get out—guns blazing—and shoot anybody who isn't me. You're my ace in the hole." *You're an ace hole all right.*

"Okay…yeah, I guess that makes sense."

"Hell, yes it does—now hop in there, soldier."

The subcontractor did as he was ordered. Then she shut the tailgate behind him and locked it. She climbed into the cab of the truck, adjusted the driver's seat, and then checked the center console, finding a protective case containing a small vial. *Oh, the vile things I could do with you*, she thought as she slipped it into her pocket.

She started up the pickup and listened to the engine rumble. *I really loathe these bumpkins, but I do love their trucks.* She navigated the large vehicle out of the parking lot, intentionally driving over several curb stops along the way.

Chapter 31

H.P. parked at the end of the broken concrete driveway of Weston's grandfather's old house. Weston had described it to him before, but clearly that description had benefited from some artistic license—this house was hardly in better condition than his own. Weston was near the garage mowing weeds, which appeared to be the only part of the lawn that was actively growing.

Weston looked up and killed the lawnmower's engine. "I'm glad you found the place."

H.P. closed the door to his nondescript car. "I thought I had the wrong house at first. I'm not accustomed to seeing you do actual work—figured you must've been someone else."

"I've got a full acre out here. You have to stay on top of the mowing or else the lawn will get away from you, though I reckon this'll probably be the last time I have to mow this year."

"A lazy guy like you with all this grass to cut...I would've thought you'd have a riding mower."

"A riding mower—what do you take me for, a fella who also sits down to pee?" Weston eyed the papers H.P. held in his hands. "I see you've brought some pages. Come on in the house and tell me about your ideas. Edwin is staying here while he gets his situation situated, but he's camped out in the shed where I keep a writing desk, trying to reconstitute his research from memory. I think the metal walls remind him of his beloved telescope. He lost all his work in the explosion, but if anyone can recall that much data, he can...never forgets a thing—has a mind like a camel."

"I think you mean an elephant."

"No, that doesn't sound right."

****

H.P. threw up his hands in exasperation. "So you don't like that one either?"

"I didn't say I didn't like it." Weston sat up in his recliner. "I didn't say anything about it."

"Well, you don't look as if you like it." H.P. tossed another batch of papers on the coffee table and leaned back into the couch.

"That's how I look all the time. I have a resting grumpy face—in addition to the fact that I currently have about a dozen Band-Aids covering my ass." Weston stood and began pacing in front of the living room's picture window. "This is good though...I feel like we're making progress."

"There's been no progress made. We're in exactly the same place as when we started. We don't have anything, and we've accomplished nothing."

"Sure we have. Don't be such a Donny Downer. We've eliminated a bunch of bad ideas, which means most of the remaining ones are bound to be good ideas. Let me hear your next one."

"Okay." H.P. sat up. "By the by 'Donny Downer' is just terrible."

"What about Robert Downer Jr.?"

"As a writer, I'm embarrassed during moments like these when the right words elude me, but what's more terrible than terrible?"

"Terribly terrible, perhaps."

"Anyway, what do you think about a scene in which the Pirate Hunter and the Spinster are being immured?"

Weston furrowed his brow. "You mean like behind a wall?"

"No, behind a butterscotch sundae. How many ways are there to be immured? Yes, of course, behind a brick wall."

"That's your idea...immursion?"

"Well, that's the start of my idea. By the by, 'immursion' isn't a word."

"By the by, faux-professor, you say 'by the by' an awful lot. I find all the 'by the bying' repetitive and repetitive. So what's the rest of it then...your idea?"

"Well, it's inchoate at present, but I thought there might be something in there worth exploring."

"Behind the wall?"

H.P. shook his head. "No, in that moment. I mean it's such a timeworn trope, but I thought we could approach it from a new angle. You know how much our characters like to prattle on. What would they say to someone immuring them?"

"Please stop?"

"Okay, so I take it you don't like this idea either."

"I didn't say that, but I'm not sure I understand where you're coming from. Shouldn't we be concerned with who's immuring them, why they're being immured, and how they'll ultimately escape their immuration rather than what they'll chat about while it's happening? I imagine it would take quite some time to build a brick wall, and then I suppose whoever did the building would want to stick around to make sure the mortar dried and hardened—that's a long time to fill with talking. I'm not sure anyone wants to read that much dialogue."

"They wouldn't have to talk the whole time."

Weston turned from the window. "What else would they do?"

"I don't know...once the wall was up, I suppose they could make love."

"Whoa, pump the brakes, Romeo. I thought we were writing some sort of adventure/mystery type story."

"Firstly, we haven't written anything yet, and secondly characters make love in those kinds of stories too...especially if they think they're about to die in a dark and secluded place. It could be very erotic."

"No, it couldn't be." Weston put his hands on his hips. "It'd likely be cold and damp...and there'd probably be spiders. Besides, I don't know what kind of smooth operator you think your Pirate Hunter is, but my Spinster isn't that type of lady. Sure, she's taken her fair share of lovers over the years, but she wouldn't lay down and roll around on the concrete floor among all the cobwebs just because she was trapped behind a wall with a guy who has a heartbeat—she'd figure out how to escape."

"Okay, we'll table the coitus conversation for now, but what do you think about this for a title: *Immurdered*. It's a portmanteau of the words 'Immured' and 'Murdered.' "

"I think it's terribly terrible, dreadfully dreadful, and horribly horrible."

"Yes, that's very constructive feedback." H.P.

leaned back again. "We've been at this for hours now, and all your haranguing has made me hungry."

"We could order a pizza. There's a place in town that'll deliver out here. Their pies aren't Chicago good, but they're not gas station bad either."

Chapter 32

She sat in the driver's seat of the truck, surveilling the house in the distance through a petite pair of binoculars with Matt sitting next to her and Brent taking up most of the backseat.

"I say we creep up behind the house when it gets a little darker, wait for him to fall asleep, and then sneak in through the back door," said Matt.

"Why don't we just kick in his front door and beat the crap out of him?" asked Brent.

She scanned the horizon and trained her binoculars on a pair of headlights in the distance. "Both great suggestions, boys, but I think I might have a better idea."

Brent turned to her. "What's that?"

She espied an illuminated pizza delivery sign affixed to the compact car's roof. "I'm going to bring him dinner and do a bit of reconnoitering."

She started up the truck, switched on its hazard lights, and pulled out from the gravel sideroad onto the blacktop, blocking both lanes.

The approaching delivery vehicle slowed to a stop. She got out of the truck and waved at the driver, walking toward his car as he rolled down his window.

"Hey, sorry to stop in the middle of the road like that, but I was just watching a bunch of deer crossing up ahead...you know how they like to move around at dusk, so I didn't want you to crash into any of them if they froze in your headlights the way they sometimes do."

"Thanks," said the driver, "that'd end my night real fast."

"Do you perchance have a delivery for Weston Payley?"

"Yeah, that's where I'm headed now. We don't usually deliver out this far, but he always tips good."

"Great, I was actually on my way there." She handed the driver a fifty-dollar bill. "You can just give me the pizza and keep the change."

"Wow...thanks." The driver took the fifty bucks and then pulled a pair of boxes out from the insulated warmer bag on the passenger seat. "Actually, it's two pizzas—a veggie supreme and a pork pleaser."

"Hmm, he must have company," she said to herself.

The driver handed her the pizzas through his window. "What's that?"

"Oh nothing." She eyed the driver's ballcap that featured the same logo as the pizza boxes. "Say, you wouldn't happen to have an extra pizza in that bag, would you? I'll throw in another fifty if you throw in your hat."

"Sure, I've got a cheese pizza and a garbage pizza."

"I don't care which. It's not for me."

"I'll give you the garbage one then." The driver took off his cap and handed it to her with the third box. "It's our most popular pizza, and this one's for a customer who never tips at all."

Chapter 33

H.P. set the penultimate batch of pages atop the pile of papers stacked on the coffee table. Then he consulted the single piece of paper that remained on the couch next to him. "All right, this is my final idea for the night."

Weston watched the darkling sky. "Then I'm confident this will prove to be an instance of saving the best for last."

"Not even close. It's sort of a macabre, mystery tale. A career criminal is so wrought with guilt—"

"Sorry," interrupted Weston, "but isn't the phrase overwrought with guilt?"

"I think it can be either."

"Are you sure?"

"I was until you brought it up. May I continue on so that we can put this one out of its misery too?"

"The mystery out of its misery." Weston smiled at the phrase. "Yes, please continue."

"The criminal feels so guilty that he hasn't been able to sleep for days. Finally, out of desperation, he consults an herbalist who has a shop on the corner. The proprietor of the bizarre store—"

"A bizarre bazaar?"

"Nope...the shopkeeper is a wise old man who is able to sense the true character of the criminal, and so he makes a sleeping concoction that actually—"

"Concoction...makes me think of a potion," Weston interrupted again. "Is that really what an herbalist does?"

"Well, these days I think herbalists mostly run marijuana dispensaries, but stick with me...I'm almost done. So the herbalist believes his—poultice, if you like—will cause the career criminal to act on his remorse and confess to his crimes, but that night the criminal sleeps more soundly than he has in months...and continues to do so night after night. However, each day the criminal is told by his underworld contacts about another former associate of his who has turned up dead. You see, the criminal has become a somnambulist, murdering the people he'd pulled jobs with in the past while he's asleep, intentionally leaving clues at the scenes of the crimes to incriminate himself."

"Not much of a mystery then, but I like the sleepwalking bit."

"Maybe we could drop the self-incrimination aspect, but here's what I think is the interesting part. Before the criminal kills each of his victims, he tells them an inexplicable yet oddly poignant story. Then he says, 'If you can guess which character you are in the story, I'll let you go free.' "

"That is interesting—so what's the inexplicable yet oddly poignant story?"

"I don't...I'm not sure." H.P. tugged on his earlobe. "I hadn't worked that part out yet."

"The whole thing sort of hinges on the story. By the way, you remind me of Carol Burnett when you do that. So would it always be the same story, or would he change it for each victim?"

"That's a good question, which I'm afraid means I don't have a good answer."

"Oh, that's okay." Weston turned back to the window. "Whenever someone says they have all the answers, it just means they don't understand all the questions. It's an intriguing idea, nonetheless."

"You don't think it's too…farfetched?"

"It's definitely farfetched, but too farfetched? I can't quite recall why we decided to have my Spinster and your Pirate Hunter team up for some sleuthing in the first place, since neither of us are really mystery writers, but as you well know, in the first modern detective story, Poe's *The Murders in the Rue Morgue*, an orangutan turns out to be the killer, so the genre lends itself to farfetchedness." Weston watched as a truck pulled into his driveway past H.P.'s car. "Anyway, it looks like our pizzas are here, so let's put a pin in this for now. Will you go out back and let the vegetarian know that his meatless dinner has arrived?"

"Sure thing." H.P. exited through the kitchen.

Weston opened the front door as a delivery driver in an ill-fitting hat climbed down from her pickup. "You could deliver a lot of pizzas with that behemoth. The usual guy drives a dinky hatchback."

"Yeah, I'm just filling in for the night." The woman approached the porch with two pizzas in hand. "These both for you?"

"No, the veggie is for a friend—frankly, I never touch the stuff."

"I hear you." She handed over the pizzas. "Well, enjoy your dinner."

"Wait—you really are new at this. What do I owe you?"

"Right." The woman turned back around. "Twenty dollars, maybe?"

"That sounds a little low." Weston pulled two twenties from his wallet. "I'll give you forty, and you can keep whatever's leftover—probably need it just to cover the cost of the gas to drive that truck all the way out here."

Chapter 34

She pulled the pickup onto the gravel sideroad. Matt and Brent were just where she'd left them, sitting out of sight of the main road, only now the open pizza box between them was mostly empty.

"We saved you a slice," Matt said.

She hopped down from the truck. "No thanks."

Matt looked up at her. "You sure? This garbage pizza is a favorite around these parts."

Before she could respond, Brent stuffed the last slice into his mouth. *I've never seen trash eat garbage before.*

Matt glared at him. "That was rude as hell."

Without ceasing his mastication, Brent growled in response. Matt reached for his holstered sidearm.

Though she was curious to see just how far these two imbeciles could escalate an argument over a slice of pizza, she thought it prudent for the sake of her operation to intercede. "As delectable as the pizza looked, I'm really not hungry, so Brent please enjoy the last slice with my compliments."

Matt checked the sights on his pistol. "Got the pre-sortie jitters, huh?"

"I guess maybe."

Brent moved from sitting to taking a knee. "So what's the play, coach?"

"Just like I figured, he's got a friend with him, so

let's incorporate both the ideas you two had into our plan."

Brent swallowed down the last of the crust. "Sounds good, but can you remind me of my idea?"

"I'll drop you two off a little ways away so as not to arouse suspicion by pulling into his driveway again. Brent, you kick in the front door, while Matthew sneaks in the back. I imagine when they see you, they'll take off running—right into the barrel of Matthew's gun. Mathew, please corral them into one of the bedrooms; Brent can assist you if either of them gets out of line."

Matt holstered his pistol. "What'll you be doing?"

My nails, perhaps. "I'll circle back and join you directly—just keep them confined to one room so they don't try to run off."

"What're we supposed to do with them?" Brent asked.

"I'll give you a roll of duct tape to keep them restrained until I get there."

Matt looked her in the eyes. "And then what?"

"Then I'll teach them a lesson they'll remember for the rest of their lives, but first we'll give them a few more minutes to finish their last meal."

"Last meal?" Matt stood up. "I thought we were just going to scare this guy."

People tend to get pretty scared right before you put a bullet in their brain. "Sorry, just a figure of speech."

Chapter 35

Weston finished off his fourth piece of pizza just as H.P. started his third. He eyed the one remaining slice in the open box on the coffee table, which by all rights belonged to H.P., and then turned his attention to the closed box next to it. *I suppose I could pick off the mushrooms.* "Did Edwin say when he was coming in? His pizza is getting cold."

"I told him it was here, and he told me he just had one last thing to finish up."

"With him, that one last thing could end up taking hours. I should've let him know there's a lantern hanging on the back wall that I sometimes use when I write out there at night."

"Why do you write in the shed at all when you've got this whole empty house?" asked H.P.

"This house isn't empty; it's full of distractions. Out there it's just me and the shovels. Where do you usually write?"

"In my attic, though I think it might be haunted, so that can be a little distracting too."

"I'd imagine so, though I suppose even when we're alone, we still have the ghosts to keep us company."

"You boys looking for some company, are you?" asked a bandanaed man, entering from the kitchen.

Weston looked up from his recliner into the barrel of a gun. "Who the hell are you?"

Before anyone could ask or answer any more questions, the front door was kicked off its hinges and a goliath ducked inside the living room.

****

Sitting in the rental truck parked in Weston's driveway, she used fast, precise strokes of the emery board to file her fingernails. After finishing all the nails on her left hand, she paused to admire her handiwork. *That looks more kempt. Now I'll do the nails on my right hand, then stroll inside to take a few pictures for the client of whatever shitshow is going on in there, next put everybody out of their misery, then take a few more pictures of the aftermath for my professional portfolio, and after that—barring any complications—I should be someplace tropical by this time tomorrow.*

Then she saw a potential complication—a light came on inside the shed in the backyard. *Now who could that be?* She put down her emery board and picked up her nine-millimeter. Her first instinct was to steal out to the shed and dispose of the complication, but then she thought better of the impulse. *It might just be a neighbor from an adjacent lot returning a borrowed weedwhacker whose wife is expecting him home momentarily. I want the police called eventually to discover the grisly scene inside, but I'd like to be the one who makes the call, preferably from an airport payphone.*

Deciding the smarter course of action would be to check on the situation inside the house first and then deal with anyone who might come knocking later, she exited the truck, walked to the porch, stepped over the front door lying on the living room carpet, and followed the sound of distraught voices to a bedroom down the hall. She opened the door to find Weston writhing on the floor, his hands bound and his mouth taped shut, which she thought suited him. The other fellow was likewise bound but up on the bed. As for her henchmen, Matt was sitting on a rocking chair near the room's only window doubled over in distress, and big Brent was in the corner of the room but amazingly still standing, though looking out of it—even for him.

Matt tried to focus his gaze on her. "What's happening to us?"

"From all appearances, nothing good," she said. "It must've been something you ate."

With excruciating effort, Matt sat up straight and attempted to extend his firearm in her direction. She studied him as he continued to exert himself.

"What did you do?" He strained to slowly raise his pistol.

"Mathew, honey, I don't think that's a very good idea. Why don't you put your gun down?"

When he'd managed to lift the pistol almost to the point where he could've taken aim at her, she quickly shot him in the head, causing the chair to rock violently backward.

"You killed your own cousin," stammered Brent.

"You saw him. He was out of his mind. A girl has to defend herself." She looked down at Weston, whose dilated pupils indicated that he was completely oblivious to what had just transpired—off in his own little world. *Too bad, I would've enjoyed being the last person he ever spoke with.* On several occasions, she'd had the opportunity to converse with her targets just before they expired and considered those brief conversations to be a unique perk of the job. She turned her attention to the man on the bed, who was very much aware of what was going on. She pulled the strip of duct tape from his mouth. "And who might you be?"

"My friends call me H.P.," he said as calmly as he could manage.

"Oh, I know who you are. Your name was in my intel as a known confrere of Weston's."

"That's correct. I take it you poisoned our pizza?"

"The drug I used was in a liquid form, so I figured the crust would soak it up nicely."

Brent steadied himself against the wall. "We ate pizza. Was it poisoned too?"

"No, darling. Why would I want to poison you? I need your help, baby."

"Yeah, that makes sense." Though Brent appeared very confused.

She looked back down at H.P. "So who's out in the shed?"

"What shed?"

She pressed the warm barrel of her gun against his temple. "No, buttercup, that's not how this game is played."

"Listen, if you have intel on me, then you know I don't live here. The truth is that today's the first time I've ever been here. If you're as clever as I think you are, then you'll know that I'm not lying."

"Maybe it's just the flattery, but I believe you." She pulled her gun away from the side of his head. "However, you make quite a cogent case for someone who should be in a nearly catatonic state by now. Either you have a constitution similar to my very large friend over there, or you didn't eat any pizza—which seems unlikely since there was only one slice left in the open box on the coffee table, and I doubt Weston ate almost the whole pie by himself—or perhaps you've been exposed to this drug before."

H.P. wondered what the Pirate Hunter would do in this situation. "The last one…at least I think so."

"Interesting." She took a seat next to him on the bed. "My client is still in the process of developing this drug, and from what I understand, it's very much a work in progress. It performs well enough, as you no doubt experienced, but the problem is that it only really works the first time—once exposed, the brain develops a kind of tolerance to it and the drug loses efficacy…and obviously repeat customers is what makes any drug profitable."

"It's a hallucinogen?"

"That's right. I've been told it's appreciably stronger than LSD…and as I understand it, the more imaginative the mind, the more elaborate the trip. The client has been testing each new iteration of its drug on unsuspecting students at the nearby university, both to see what it might do to creative young minds and because they figure any bad trips will be dismissed as the result of yet another recreational drug on the college campus."

"What'll it do to my friend?"

"Without medical attention, the amount he ingested would most likely cause irreparable insanity, but don't worry—he won't suffer long."

Before H.P. could fully consider the implications of her last statement, a fiery flash lit up the area outside the bedroom window. She quickly crossed the room to see her pickup truck ablaze in the driveway, from which she thought issued the sound of a faint screaming. Brent looked to her for guidance, seeming unsure if any of this was really happening.

"What are you looking at me for…go check it out."

Brent lumbered out of the bedroom. Then from the hallway, the reverberating sound of something metal striking something hard could be heard, followed by the loud thud of a heavy object hitting the floor. A moment later Edwin entered the bedroom holding a shovel. She pointed her gun at his face, and he dropped the shovel.

"I heard the gunshot," Edwin said as he surveyed the room. "I was hoping the big guy in the hall was the one who'd fired it."

"No such luck." She motioned for Edwin to sit on the corner of the bed next to H.P. "So you set my truck on fire? It's okay…it was just a rental."

"I saw the sticker on the back bumper," said Edwin. "The same one that was on the abandoned sedan from last night, so I smashed a lantern against it. You're the one who hit me over the head and blew up my telescope, right?"

"Yep, though it wasn't technically your telescope, now was it? So we've each destroyed something that didn't actually belong to the other—no big loss. I don't suppose you happened to see a fella emerge from underneath that tonneau cover when you set fire to the truck."

"There was someone under there?"

"Yeah, but again—no big loss. I was probably going to kill him anyway."

H.P. looked up at her. "Just like you intend to kill us, I'll wager."

"Why would you wager on that?" Edwin asked.

"That's a good question. Yes, H.P., you'd win that

136

bet, but then of course lose your life, though I hadn't planned to start that portion of our evening right away; however, even all the way out here, a burning truck in the front yard won't go unnoticed for long, so I suppose I ought to expedite these proceedings. Edwin, I think I'll stage the scene with you in the role of the would-be hero coming to the rescue of your friends. You knock out the sasquatch in the hallway—kudos for that by the way—then rush in here to free these two, failing to notice the crazed gun store owner laying in wait in the corner of the room...in a rocking chair. H.P. you're a writer—can one lay in wait while sitting?"

"Yes and no." H.P. twisted around on the bed to get a better look at the occupant of the rocking chair. "One does not 'lay in wait' but rather 'lies in wait'; however, one need not be lying down to do so."

"That's good to know." She reached down to aim the dead man's pistol in Edwin's direction, all while keeping her own gun in her other hand trained on him too.

Edwin held up his hands. "Hold on. How will you account for the bullet in his head if he shoots me? Shouldn't I be holding your gun?"

"Easy, cowboy, this isn't my first rodeo." *I've been here for too long—now I'm starting to talk like a yokel.* "I'll wipe my prints off the gun, then put it in the sasquatch's hand for a moment, and then finally—after you're dead, for obvious reasons—in yours so it'll look like a simultaneous shooting...bing, bang, boom."

As if to punctuate her *boom*, the truck in the driveway exploded, blowing in the window and bombarding the room with glass and debris. Edwin and H.P. were thrown from the bed and covered by the mattress that flipped over on top of them. Edwin gathered his wits and then pushed the mattress off. The bedroom's outer wall was consumed by flames, and the window was now a floor-to-ceiling hole. A smoldering corpse lay face down in the middle of the room. Fearing it was Weston, Edwin turned the body over to discover that it was the dead man who'd been in the rocking chair. Then he saw that Weston had been blown into the hallway. Edwin pulled H.P. into the hall and then dragged both him and Weston out the back door. Once outside and at a safe distance from the burning house, he stopped to catch his breath.

As he gasped for air, Edwin started to peel away the tape restraining H.P. "Trust me...I know how this feels." He heard distant sirens and scanned his surroundings. In the moonless night, far beyond the shed, he could just make out a shadowy figure slipping into the woods.

Chapter 36

Weston talked with Rebecca, but it wasn't his Becca, and somehow it wasn't him either. He couldn't hear what either of them were saying, as if he were watching himself and her through a soundproof window. She appeared frantic to tell him something important. Suddenly she turned from the Weston in the room to the Weston in the window.

Weston awoke in near darkness. It was raining outside. He looked around to get his bearings and sensed that someone else was with him. "Who's there?"

"Hey sport, it's me." Slim sat up in the chair by the hospital bed. "Becky just left to drop the kids off at her sister's, but she'll be back real soon. Strictly speaking, I ain't technically supposed to be in here, since I'm not family, but then for that matter neither is Becky…technically."

"That's an oversight on my part that I now see is in need of remedying."

"You ain't asking to marry me, is you?"

Weston chuckled, but it made his stomach hurt. "No, that's not the proposal I had in mind. How long have I been out?"

"Two days…they put you under sedation just as I was coming off of it—had you on a drip of a few different medications that I can't hardly pronounce as well as what they call a gastrointestinal

139

decontamination protocol using activated charcoal. I offered the doc some of the briquettes from my grill at home, but she told me they had it all under control. How do you feel?"

"Like I've been dreaming nonstop for a week...but that I still need more sleep." Weston reached for the water cup on the side table. "How are you feeling?"

Slim poured some ice water from a pitcher into the cup and then handed it to Weston. "Still a little sluggish from that slug I took, but I'll be fine."

"And the others?"

"Your friend Edwin is a bit shaken from having almost been killed two nights in a row, which is understandable, and H.P. is—well—pissed off...he can be downright ornery for a bookish sort. He's been working tirelessly with my department for the past couple days, trying to track down your pizza lady and her client."

"Any headway?"

"None as of yet. The car from the telescope and the truck from your house were both rented through the same corporate account. Apparently, the rental agency doesn't do much in the way of vetting its corporate clients as long as they pay their bills in a timely manner, so that's led nowhere. We have some vague descriptions of this gal—mostly that she's comely and probably not from around here...otherwise she's pretty much a ghost. Bits of bone fragments were found in and around your driveway, indicating that there was likely some poor soul trapped in the truck when it blew, but as close as we've gotten to IDing the individual is that it was somebody who had bones. As for the two burned bodies we took out of your place, they've been IDed—

one was a local gun nut, and the other was an outlaw biker type...both them boys were known to my department."

"There was a fire at my house?"

"Oh right, they told me you were pretty out of it for that part."

"Was there much damage?"

"Uhm, on the upside, that fire—in a roundabout kinda way—most likely saved your life; on the downside everything above the foundation is ash and cinders."

Weston tried to recall the last thing he remembered about his granddad's house, but no specific recollections came to mind, just a general feeling that the house had been a part of his life for a long time. "I suppose there's no sense in dwelling on a dwelling that I hardly ever stayed at anymore—ah well, more's the pity."

"When we get out of here, I think you and me both deserve some rest and relaxation so as to fully recuperate."

"You mean fishing, don't you?"

Slim smiled. "I do indeed."

Chapter 37

Hitchhiking with her face half blown off had been a challenge, though not nearly as difficult as the self-surgery in her motel bathroom proved to be. She'd had to make several incisions with the blade from a box cutter that she'd filched from a truckdriver in order to dig out the shards of glass embedded in the side of her face. She'd been lucky that she hadn't caught any glass in her eye, though 'lucky' was not a word she felt accurately described her current circumstances.

I should be on a beach right now, but instead I'm in yet another disgusting motel room, which was paid for with the two twenties Weston gave me. She lay in bed, staring up at the dust caked blades of the ceiling fan. She inhaled and exhaled deeply in an attempt to breathe through the waves of throbbing pain. Sleep had come in fits and starts, which wasn't beneficial for convalescing but did afford her frequent opportunities to change her makeshift bandages.

Having been awoken for the umpteenth time by a honking semi on the highway just outside her door, she got out of bed and tottered into the bathroom. In the grimy mirror, she inspected her wounds. The cuts had stopped bleeding, and some of the puffiness was now gone, both of which were encouraging signs, but the bruising on her face had started to change color from pinks and reds to purples and blues.

Maybe I could pass for a battered wife on the run, or I could shave my head and try to pass for a man. She figured she'd have to shave her head soon enough anyway for the plastic surgery that she would inevitably need. She liked her face...or at least she did, but she'd lived with it long enough that she didn't mind the prospect of a change, though she'd heard stories from her mentor when she was first starting out in the business about older hitwomen who'd undergone plastic surgery once they retired, and they looked good—younger even, but as they aged their faces took on an unnatural appearance.

She cautiously washed her face and patted it dry with a scratchy, threadbare towel. She hadn't decided yet if it would be better to visit her mother and sister before she got her new face, so they could see it one last time, such as it was, or wait until after the surgery so as to spare them the sight of her latest scars—and maybe even make her sister a little jealous of her new look. Either way, she'd have to invent a story that could hold up to a thousand different questions about what had happened, though she knew she had time, since it would likely be a while before she'd see them again.

She returned to bed and turned on the television. She was always curious to see how many states away the local news would give accounts of her exploits. Once, a high-profile hit of hers made the national news, but that had been a long time ago. The last news item she'd heard about her latest assignment mentioned that the local writer whose house had burned down was expected to make a full recovery, but she'd crossed three state lines since then, and she hadn't heard any further updates. If only her association-issued computer hadn't been in the truck when it blew. If only she didn't have to go all the way back home for her spare laptop to check in with her handler. If only…

Soon the sound of the TV and the sound of the traffic outside receded into the background and sleep began to overtake her weary body once again. As her eyes closed, she pictured Weston bound on the floor just as he had been before the explosion eroded her face. Logically, she knew it'd been her own fault for lingering too long—she'd seen it enough times before, *all burning vehicles eventually become bombs*—but still, incapacitated as he'd been, she somehow blamed him. He would make a full recovery, and she'd been disfigured. Now she understood why her client hated him so much. As she drifted off to sleep, she imagined putting her heel on Weston's throat and delivering the coup de grâce that would've completed her assignment.

Chapter 38

After a full night's sleep unaided by sedatives, Weston felt considerably better. Even the hospital food they brought him for breakfast mostly tasted good. He expected to be discharged later in the morning and was looking forward to what the remainder of the day might offer.

Becky pulled back the semitransparent curtain covering the window, which changed the ambient light in the room from pleasant to punishing. "Since you're already here, I'm going to see about rescheduling your colonoscopy before they let you go."

Weston set down his little cup of orange juice on the tray next to his bed. "I've just gone through a very harrowing experience. Aren't I entitled to a respite before embarking on another?"

"First of all, tough guy, you were unconscious for most of your latest 'experience,' and secondly, a routine medical procedure hardly qualifies as harrowing. Besides, you're already wearing an assless gown."

"I'll thank you not to remind me of that fact." Weston pushed the button to adjust his bed to a more horizontal position in hopes that the sight of a supine man in a hospital room might arouse some compassion in the stone-hearted woman. "Although I do appreciate that there's less friction on the Band-Aids covering my backside."

"No, the nurse took those off while you were unconscious."

"Someone touched my butt while I was asleep?"

"Oh, get over it."

"Was it that male nurse or a female?"

"Which would be better?"

"There's no better—only worse. If you're so keen on me having a colonoscopy—which I find sadistic, by the way—why didn't you just have them do it while I was under?"

Before Becky could answer, there was a knock at the door. "Is everyone decent?" Slim entered the room. "I sure hope not."

Becky shook her head. "Saved by the dumbbell."

"Slim, you're wearing street clothes."

"Yeah, the doc just gave me my walking papers— felt good to pull on my boots again. I heard that you'll be getting out of here soon too."

"Not if Becca has her way. She thinks I need some more poking and prodding."

"Aw now, Miss Becky, it ain't good for a man to be cooped up indoors for too long."

"Well, I guess when it comes to sound medical advice, it's *slim* pickings around here."

"I see what you did there with my name and all."

"I need to go take the boys to school." Becky kissed Weston and then headed for the door. "But I'll be back soon, and we're going to talk more about that procedure."

Weston positioned himself upright in bed again. "I thought that woman would never leave."

"I take it you ain't gotten around to asking her to marry you yet."

"Did I say that?"

"Last night when you first woke up."

"I was probably still under the influence of all the drugs they had me on. Speaking of things that we may or may not have talked about yesterday, I've been trying to puzzle through everything you told me before Becky came back and shooed you out of here last night, and I was hoping you could answer a few questions to get me up to speed."

Slim took a seat. "Fire away."

"So this pizza lady sounds like a real serious operator. Do you think she could've been the one who shot you?"

"That's what we sort of figured. I didn't get a look at the shotgunner who got the drop on me, but somebody big wouldn't have fit inside the trunk of that Mustang."

"Could she have also been the one who blew up the telescope?"

"Edwin thinks so, based on the brief confab he had with her at your place."

"So in each case, she had an accomplice—a chauffeur to drive the Mustang, and then someone who tailed her to the telescope. Your cop buddies must've shown you the mugshot of the fellow they have in custody—the owner of the Mustang."

Slim nodded. "As a matter of fact, they did. He wasn't the one driving the night I pulled that car over, so they cut him loose yesterday, though I think it'll be safer for everybody if we keep his hotrod locked up for a little while longer."

"I'm glad they let him go...I never liked him for it."

"Is that right?"

"I did a little investigating on my own—"

"H.P. mentioned as much…filled me in on your investigation, which sounds like involved a fair amount of drinking."

"Well, we had to blend in…you know, undercover like."

"I'm sure no one was the wiser," said Slim.

"So the bits of bone from whoever was in the truck when it exploded—could that have been the driver of the Mustang? Maybe pizza lady Mickeyed the car's owner at the Boutonniere, which wouldn't have taken much since it sounds as if he was half in the bag already. Then, with the help of her accomplice, they drop him off unconscious at his trailer and next go gunning for you. Perhaps later, for whatever reason, they decide to switch roles at my house, but before he gets to do his part, Edwin sets the truck on fire, which eventually ignites the fuel tank."

"It all fits, and I prefer that scenario a whole lot more than one where some innocent hostage gets blown to pieces, but I don't think we'll ever know for certain. After telling me what you two were up to, I told H.P. the details, as best I could, about our caper out at the shooting club this past winter. In fact, I called him last night after you and I talked to let him know you were awake, and he was awful anxious to share with you a theory involving some peculiar goings-on he's been dealing with of late—mentioned he'd planned to stop by first thing this morning, so I'll let you get the story straight from him rather than relaying it second hand. Suffice it to say, I think you boys might've stumbled into different ends of the same briar patch without even knowing it."

"He told me the same thing last night." H.P. stood in the doorway, holding a bouquet of flowers.

Weston eyed the bouquet. "Who are the flowers for? I'm not dead."

"I thought they might brighten up the room a little. Where should I put them?"

"Back from wherever you got them. I'm not your damn prom date."

H.P. carefully set the bouquet on the table near the bed. "You can give them to Becky when you propose."

Weston looked at Slim over the flowers. "Well, you just tell everybody everything, don't you?"

"He wanted to know what you had to say when you first woke up."

"I've been thinking about this whole briar patch thing," said H.P. "I figure the pizza lady's client that's behind the hallucinogens students are being slipped on campus is probably the same organization behind the drug plot you uncovered at the work farm."

Slim leaned back in his chair. "Seems likely...or at least possible, but we never got anywhere with finding out who they were. Both the rangemaster and Dr. Weize went missing from this very hospital the day after they arrived, then their bodies were found later out in a pond at the shooting club, which closed shop soon afterward."

"Right, I inquired about Dr. Weize on campus, but his department members were as reluctant to talk about him as folks in my department are to talk about a colleague who also recently disappeared. In addition, I made inquiries about the vendors who supply the cafeterias on campus, but all I got were vague answers and minimal cooperation."

Slim folded his arms. "That angle was worth a try, but if this lady could dose some pizzas on the fly, then anybody could dose just about anything in a cafeteria."

H.P. looked up at the ceiling. "I suppose so. If only we had a sample of the drug she used."

"Unfortunately, greasy pizzas and the oleaginous boxes that contain them are flammable," Weston said. "I'm sure all the evidence was burned."

Slim stood up. "I'm going to step out into the hallway to make a quick call."

H.P. took a seat in the vacated chair. "Do you recall anything distinctive about the pizza lady?"

"From what Slim told me, it sounds like you gave the same description as what I remember...as did everyone else who saw her—from the actual pizza delivery guy to the employees at the motels she stayed at."

"Right, but there must be something we're missing."

"This isn't one of our stories—clues don't just present themselves and lead neatly back to the villain."

H.P. touched the tips of his fingers together. "I know, but still...I can't help but think there has to be a loose thread to pull at. Did you notice if she had an accent?"

"I didn't notice any at all."

"Me neither, which is strange...I mean everyone has some sort of accent, don't they?"

"She's a pro. She's probably been trained not to speak with an accent, but what are you asking me for? It sounds like you talked to her a lot more than I did. Did she say anything to you that hit your ear funny?"

"I've been replaying our conversation over and over in my mind, but nothing stands out."

"Keep at it...everyone, even a ghost, leaves behind footprints—just some are bigger than others."

H.P. rubbed his chin. "Bigger footprints."

"What are you mumbling about?"

"Bigfoot."

"If we can't catch her, I don't think we stand much chance of catching him."

"No, she called that giant who kicked in your door a sasquatch—not bigfoot."

"Okay, so..."

"So in Canada bigfoots are called sasquatches."

"And you think that makes her Canadian?" asked Weston. "That's pretty thin, and it doesn't do much to narrow our search."

"Maybe, but at least it's something."

Slim reentered the room. "Well boys, I can't get you a pizza, but I can get you a pizza box. One of our detectives found a greasy cardboard box from the same pizzeria on a sideroad near your house—seems the bad guys had a picnic before they stopped by your place and didn't bother to clean up after themselves."

"And that's something else," said H.P.

Chapter 39

She'd made it back to her apartment just in time not to miss her third daily check-in call. She quickly pulled the bag from under her bed that contained her spare association computer. She wished she had time to shower and change into presentable clothes, but this was to be the final meeting before the association wrote her off completely, in which case she'd have to go through the long, tortuous process of reestablishing contact, provided they would even have an associate back after missing three calls in a row.

She plugged in the laptop and opened it, quickly typing in her access code as soon as the screen came to life. It took a few moments to establish a secure connection, but then she heard the same familiar phrase that began each call, "How are you today?" Though even the digitized voice seemed skeptical of a response.

"As well as can be expected," she answered.

The encryption delay felt longer than usual. She didn't like to think such thoughts, but it was possible that the association would be disappointed to learn she was still alive and take measures to ensure that she didn't stay that way.

"Well hello there—I'm so pleased that you're still with us. I'd hoped for the best, of course, since there was no report of a female body being recovered at—oh my, yes the video feed is coming through now, and I see that you did not escape unscathed."

"Just a few scratches that'll probably require some minor surgery."

If only I had time to put on makeup. The bruises were now mostly green and yellow, easily concealable, especially over video, but then there were still the cuts and burns.

"Yes, surgery is definitely in your future. It looks like you're back home, so I'll email you some contacts for talented plastic surgeons in your area who've shown a great deal of discretion when working with some of our other associates in the past."

"Thanks, that would be helpful."

Or not—what better way to dispose of me than to schedule an off-the-books operation that I never wake up from?

"We'll continue our daily calls to maintain your active status, but for now I just want you to focus on getting fixed up."

"Wait, the job's not done yet. I want to be put back in play. I could've completed my assignment by now, if I didn't have to hightail it home in order to keep in contact."

Check your tone…don't make the decision to terminate your employment or your life easy for them.

"We appreciate your enthusiasm, but even if we thought it a good idea to send you back out into the field right now, the client feels there's too much heat for the time being to continue on."

"Then are there any other jobs available? I know I don't look my best at the moment, but I could still manage a sniper assignment, and I'm itching to get back to work."

Figures the client would develop cold feet when things got a little hot, but I think we'd all sleep better if Weston was permanently out of the picture.

"Negative, your looks—your ability to get in close—are what makes you such a valuable asset. The association is contacted by a dozen or more applicants a week who are qualified to shoot at a target from across the street. We need you in a business suit not a ghillie suit. Get better, and then we'll talk about getting you back out there."

"If that's the priority then, there's a spa nearby that'd really help to accelerate my convalescence—thing is they don't allow any tech, strictly bathrobes and flipflops. They take all your personal effects when you check in. Now that I've updated you on my situation, if you could clear me from say a week's worth of check-in calls, I could get back in the game that much faster."

She imagined her heel on Weston's throat again. *They don't have to pay me to punch your ticket; I'll be glad to do it for free...seems like soon I'll have some time to kill.*

Chapter 40

H.P. held the door to the neurobiology department open for Weston, who entered with the soiled pizza box in hand.

Weston surveyed the high-tech lab through a long window in the hallway. "This place is way nicer than your dumpy old English Building."

H.P. knocked on the door to the dean's office. "I should warn you, she can be a little prickly, so keep on your best behavior."

"Don't worry...I have an effect on women."

"Come," the dean's voice instructed. H.P. and Weston entered. "Ah, it's you again—so what have you brought me today to examine...a pizza?"

"Not exactly," Weston answered for H.P.

"And you must be the colleague who's concerned he's being poisoned?"

"No," H.P. replied. "This is my friend Weston Payley, he's a—"

"I know who he is...you wrote *Serotonergic Spinster*, didn't you?"

Weston smiled. "Yes ma'am, that's correct."

"What an unmitigated piece of claptrap that turned out to be. Tell me, did you do any research into the field of neuroscience whatsoever before writing that book? Not even the title made sense."

"I'm sorry you didn't enjoy it," Weston said.

"I didn't say that exactly. I found it rather amusing…a good diversion from what can sometimes be the rather uptight and punctilious world of neurobiology. So what can I do for you two today?"

H.P. took the empty box from Weston and opened it to show the dean. "This box contained a pizza we know to have been dosed with a hallucinogen. The liquid drug was poured onto the crust of what was a very greasy pizza, as you can see from the box's condition."

"So you're hoping my team will be able to isolate and analyze any runoff from the drug that might've gotten trapped in the grease. It's a good idea, and I hate to disappoint, but that's just not how it works. For an analysis to be of any value, we'd need an unadulterated sample, and we can't isolate a sample captured in a coagulant if we don't know what we're looking for. It'd be like trying to find a needle in a haystack if you'd never seen a needle before."

"Is there anyone who might be able to help us?" asked Weston.

H.P. rubbed his forehead. "What about that behavioral neuroscientist you mentioned the other day? The one who did a fellowship?"

"You're talking about Kate," Weston said, "Edwin's old squeeze."

"They were together? I didn't realize he liked women…or anyone."

"Sorry to interrupt your little gossip session, but Kate moved on to a very lucrative position with a biotech conglomerate headquartered in the Chicago suburbs. She's the only person I can think of who might be able to help you, especially given the equipment at her disposal now, which is all the absolute bleeding edge compared to what we have here; however, from what I understand they keep her rather busy."

Weston whistled softly. "So her lab is more state-of-the-art than this place?"

"By comparison, hers makes our facility look like state-of-the-finger-painting."

"And the offices here are like a thousand times better than what you have in your subterranean department," Weston said to H.P. "Does the university even pay you guys?"

H.P. hustled Weston out into the hallway and waved to the dean. "Thanks again for your time."

Chapter 41

As the two walked across the quad, H.P. noticed furtive glances from some of the students they passed, though he could not definitively ascribe the attention they were receiving to any one cause—perhaps he and Weston stood out because they were so much older than everyone else around them, or maybe they were being recognized as two quasi-famous writers, but it might've been that they were carrying a malodorous pizza box.

"We need to find a big plastic bag for this thing." H.P. tried to hand the box to Weston. "It's starting to stink."

"I don't want it," Weston said.

"But it's your turn."

"It's my turn to carry an empty box that stinks?"

"That's right, we're in this thing together."

Weston reluctantly took the pizza box and held it as high above his head as his outstretched arm would allow.

"What in the world are you doing?" asked H.P.

"I'm trying to keep our evidence as far away from my nose as possible."

"If you're so sensitive about your nose, why don't you hold the evidence down at your side?"

"This sidewalk is crowded—someone might bump into it and smear grease on my pants."

"You look like a damn fool."

"I'd look all the more foolish with greasy trousers," said Weston.

"So do you know this Kate?"

"I only met her once."

"The dean seemed to think a great deal of her abilities, but was she otherwise impaired or something?"

"I don't think so. I found her to be quite charming."

H.P. shook his head. "I just don't understand it…I mean can you imagine Edwin asking her for a date? 'Hey, do you want to see my telescope, or how about my comprehensive collection of *Fantastic Four* comic books?' "

"I think you're underestimating Edwin. He can be a charmer too when he wants to be."

"Well, it looks like we're going to need his help, so I hope he can turn on the charm and get us an appointment with his ex."

"I have no doubt that he'll be happy to oblige."

"Where is Prince Charming now, anyway?"

"He's staying at Becca's place, and it sounds like he's been driving everybody nuts."

Chapter 42

Weston opened the front door to Becky's house, then he and H.P. stepped into pandemonium. Becky held a screaming baby as she chased Lance, who ran past with a fragile, sci-fi looking gizmo, while Van sat on the couch, studying a stack of star charts on the coffee table and listening to rap music at a deafening decibel.

Weston turned off the stereo and then grabbed Lance as he ran by again. Becky soon reentered the living room in pursuit, and Ance quieted down when her mother came to a stop.

"Hey, I was listening to that," said Van.

Lance squirmed in Weston's grasp. "Let go."

Becky put a hand on her hip. "Where have you been?"

"Let's all take a deep breath." Weston demonstrated an exaggerated inhalation. "Now everybody hold that breath for fifteen minutes. Van, the way you feel about my music is the way the rest of us feel about yours, so listen to it on your headphones or in your room and keep the volume below an eardrum-splitting level. Lance, I'll let go of you, if you let go of whatever it is that you've got there."

"No, it's my new toy—finders keepers."

"Okay, if you can tell me what it does or what it's called, I'll let you keep it."

Lance studied the gadget for a moment and then handed it over.

"Thanks, now go on up to your room and play with your robots." Weston turned to Becky and stroked his baby daughter's downy hair. "I'm sorry, we were on campus following up on a clue that might lead us to whoever burned down my house, but I should've called."

"Yeah, you should've. I was worried...and overwhelmed. Your friend has his electronic thingamajigs all over my dining room table, which as you saw are way too tempting for Lance; he also has his dirty laundry piled up on my washer, which if he thinks I'm going to do it then he's got another thing coming; and for some reason his shoes are in the microwave. Meanwhile, he's sequestered himself in the garage and only comes out when he's hungry."

"Of course, he doesn't think you're going to do his laundry." Weston kissed Becky's forehead. "I'll talk to him about cleaning up the table...and the microwave."

"I thought all his stuff blew up, but he keeps bringing in more junk."

"He's probably been going through his things at his storage unit in town to see what he can use to continue his work."

"A storage unit...can he live there?"

"He can stay with me for a while," H.P. said, "now that he's had a chance to gather the items he needs."

"Thank you." Becky smiled. "That would be a huge help."

Edwin entered from the garage. "Will dinner be ready soon?"

****

H.P. looked over the pages and pages of data spread out on the ping pong table in the garage. "You did all this from memory…just in the last few days?"

"Don't touch any of that," said Edwin. "There's a system at work there."

"I don't doubt it."

Weston eyed a blink comparator in an open box. "You once told me that everything is chemistry."

"Yes, I recall."

"Well, we think we have a clue that only an expert chemist could help us with."

"I don't claim to be an expert, but I do have a spare microscope in storage that I could—"

"No, I think we'll need equipment a little more advanced than that," Weston said, "operated by someone with a bit more expertise."

"You could try over at the university."

"We just came from the neurobiology department." H.P. tapped an orrery. "The dean couldn't help us, but she thought someone named Kate could."

"Your Kate," said Weston, "or rather your erstwhile Kate."

"You two want me to call my ex for a favor…on top of just having saved both your lives the other night?"

Weston turned his attention from the comparator. "Well, I did save your life the night before that, and this clue might help us find whoever it was that blew up your telescope. Besides, doesn't H.P. look so sad and pathetic. Don't you want to help that miserable guy be happy again?"

H.P. looked up from the orrery, appearing confused by all the fuss.

"Now that you mention it, he does look rather pitiful," said Edwin. "I suppose I could make a call, though talking to her again is going to be a lot more difficult than dragging you two out of a burning building."

"Thanks, and one more thing—could you get your damn shoes out of the microwave?"

Chapter 43

Her plane had touched down over an hour ago, but she was only just pulling out of the airport car rental lot. She missed the perks of her corporate credit card, which availed her of the express rental program, but she dared not tip her hand to the association of where she really was. At least she'd be able to stay in nicer accommodations during this visit.

However, before she checked into a hotel, she needed to purchase a suitable sidearm, which on the secondary market would likely be less time-consuming than renting a car. She'd researched several options while waiting in the rental line. During the flights home after an assignment, she sometimes thought back on all the guns she'd bought over her career that she'd had to toss into a dumpster or drop down a sewer grate soon after a job was completed, and it made her melancholy. They had been useful tools that deserved a better fate than being buried in a landfill or rusting in a cesspool. If she had her druthers, she'd proudly display them as souvenirs of her heretofore flawless record, though of course that would be a terrible idea for so many reasons. Still, the thought of having a memento of her exploits that she could look back on if and when she retired held an appeal.

Maybe I could make an exception just this once, she thought as she drove her rental car into a supermarket parking lot, *and have the disassembled pieces of the gun I use to kill Weston shipped to me*. She knew even entertaining such a notion meant that this job—which was no longer technically a job, but rather sport hunting—had become too personal, but though it was unprofessional, she felt justified in thinking this one meant a little more. She'd never had an assignment end unsuccessfully or sustained such a grievous injury.

She spotted the cargo van the seller had described parked in an empty area of the lot far away from the store. *This idiot should just slap on a bumper sticker that reads: Illicit Merchandise Inside*. She parked next to the van, and the driver rolled down his passenger-side window as she rolled down hers.

The driver, who had sideburns that extended to his mustache, leaned across the van's empty passenger seat. "You the lady who emailed me about that pistol?"

"Yes I am."

"You're not a cop, are you? You'd have to tell me if you was."

"No, I wouldn't, but I'm not." She turned to look at him so that he could see the fresh scars and blisters on the other half of her face.

"Yeah, okay...I guess you wouldn't be working undercover with your face looking that way. What is it—you want to get even with the person who did that to you?"

"Something like that. Now let me see the gun."

"Sure, I've got it here in the back...hop in."

She considered the idea for a moment. *I could just cut his throat and let him bleed out back there while I loot his inventory; I'm already out a substantial sum of my own money on this trip, and the world won't miss one more sleazeball.* However, the surveillance camera affixed to a nearby light pole caused her to reconsider that line of thinking. "There's no way I'm getting in your creepy ass van—just toss me the gun through the window."

"What if you drive off?"

Since when did low-rent arms dealers become so untrusting? "Life is risk, but I'll tell you what: I've got your money in this bag. I'll take out half, then throw you the bag. You take out the money and count it, then put the gun in and toss the bag back. I'll inspect the gun, and if I like what I see, I'll throw the bag back with the other half of the money, and then finally you toss me the bullets."

"Okay, I guess that would work."

"Sure, it will." *Sometimes I wish I'd gone into dentistry.*

Chapter 44

Edwin had just finished moving his scientific doodads from the dining room table into the garage when Weston returned with several sacks of takeout food.

Becky held Ance as she corralled Lance and Van into the dining room. "What, did you order like one of everything?"

Weston set the bags on the table. "Yeah, was that a mistake? We've never tried this place before, so we don't know what's good there."

"And if none of it's good, we've got one of everything," said Lance.

Edwin entered from the garage. "Did I hear Weston pull up with the food?"

H.P. emerged from the kitchen with six glasses in hand. "What smells so good?"

"A new Thai restaurant opened up in town that we've been meaning to try." Weston began taking small containers out of the bags.

H.P. distributed the glasses around the table. "I'm envious. We don't have a Thai place around campus. There was briefly a Vietnamese establishment that served a very tasty pho, but it soon went out of business. Our only other Asian options are a pricey sushi spot and a few Chinese restaurants that all taste about the same."

Becky took out six plates from the sideboard. "I have little doubt that if our town's new Thai place wants to stay open, they'll have to add General Tso's chicken to the menu by the end of the month."

Van sat down next to Edwin. "You're a stars and planets guy, so I've been meaning to ask you—I know this girl at school who wants to study astrology. Do you have any advice for her?"

"Never have children," answered Edwin.

Weston retrieved a water pitcher and a jug of chocolate milk from the kitchen as the rest of the dinner party took their seats. Then the doorbell rang. "I'm up, so let me get it." Weston placed the pitcher and the jug on the table. He opened the front door to find Slim standing on the porch.

"I hope I'm not interrupting your supper," said Slim.

"As a matter of fact, we just sat down to eat. You're welcome to join us. We ordered a bunch of food from that new Thai restaurant."

"What's that like, pretzels and garlic knots?"

Weston had gotten to know Slim fairly well over the past year, but he still couldn't always tell when Slim was genuinely being a rube and when he was just acting the part. "Not really, but considering all the different sorts of critters you hunt and cook, I'm sure we can find you something to whet your appetite."

"Thanks just the same, but I'm on my way to pick up my boy for pizza; however, I wanted to stop by to let you know that I heard back from my contact at the NTSB."

"About a Canadian woman flying into the airport near campus after purchasing a last-minute ticket? The lead you thought was too preposterous to bother pursuing—even though H.P. and I argued, how many people would make last-minute international travel plans to fly into a tiny Midwestern airport?"

"The one and the same, and just for the record, I still think it's preposterous, though now that I say that out loud, 'preposterous' sounds more like a you word than a me word. Anyway, I reckon the lady I got the tip about probably flew in for some egghead emergency at the college, but just in case I'm wrong I wanted to let you know that one Allison Belched landed earlier today. Mid-thirties like you all described. The hair color and eye color on her passport don't match your description, but then those can be changed for a picture."

"Maybe we can find out where she's staying," said Weston. "Has she used any credit cards since she arrived?"

"I couldn't say. My contact is only hooked into the passport database. Tracking credit cards is a whole different level, and I ain't got no friends at that paygrade, but it probably wouldn't do us much good anyhow. If this lady really is the bad gal we all ran afoul of, she's likely got multiple credit cards in different names, since those are easier to come by than a phony passport, so long as somebody keeps making the payments."

"I appreciate you letting me know."

"You bet. I already informed my department, so don't be surprised if you see a patrol car driving by here a few dozen times tonight, but like I told you before, it probably ain't her. I mean it'd be downright unprofessional to return to the scene of the crime, so to speak, and this gal seems smart enough not to do something so…preposterous, but then you're pretty smart, and I seen you do plenty of preposterous shit."

Weston was unsure if Slim was being sincere about the compliment or sarcastic about the criticism— probably both, he figured. "Thanks for stopping by, Slim."

"10-4, just stay put and keep your head down for the next few days while we continue our investigation—but there's probably nothing to be concerned about, so don't make yourself crazy by thinking there's a sniper hiding in every bush…and enjoy them Pad Thai noodles."

Chapter 45

Allison surveilled the house of one Rebecca Hernandez from beneath a bush on a knoll far across the road. With her high-powered binoculars, she could see several people through the windows moving about inside, but she'd yet to locate her target.

She'd checked with the hospital and discovered that Weston had already been discharged. The intel she'd received on him indicated that he'd recently had a baby with "Becky," so Allison figured that since his house had been destroyed it stood to reason that he would be staying here. She'd also just seen the fourth police car drive past in the last half hour, and there wasn't much else around, so she surmised that they must be keeping an eye on this house for a reason.

The front door opened, and two men exited, saying their goodbyes from the porch and blocking her view inside the house. Allison identified the two leaving as H.P. and Edwin—and then she finally saw Weston standing in the doorway. She considered sprinting back to her car, running the two off the road a mile or so away, putting a bullet in each of their heads, and then circling back for Weston, but with the heightened police presence in the area, Allison knew there'd be a risk of a cop happening by the scene, forcing her to flee and delaying the final kill. When the police discovered Weston's two friends murdered, they'd likely take him into protective custody, which meant she wouldn't get another shot at him for maybe months...if ever.

No, Weston is the only target that really matters—to me and the client.

Allison looked on as H.P. and Edwin loaded a few things from the garage into the trunk of a car parked in the driveway and then drove off together. She continued to surveil the house as Weston cleaned up what remained of dinner. He walked back and forth from the kitchen to the dining room, while two boys watched television in the living room. Allison wondered about Becky's whereabouts—then a light came on upstairs in what looked to be the master bedroom.

Allison focused in turn on each of the rooms where there was activity, attempting to establish a pattern so that she could predict what might happen next. She noticed a crib near the bedroom window, but Rebecca was nursing in bed. She looked exhausted, so Allison figured she was done for the night. She watched as the boys began to tussle over the remote control on the couch, then Weston appeared to say something to them from the dining room. Given the lateness of the hour, she suspected it was getting close to the boys' bedtime.

To Allison's dismay, another police car slowly drove past the house, momentarily obstructing her view and potentially hindering her plan. *Is he like a friend of the police chief, or something?* The dining table now cleared, she watched as Weston entered the living room and shooed the boys off the couch. They went upstairs, but no lights came on from the second floor that she could see, so she deduced that their bedrooms must be at the back of the house. Allison saw Becky get out of bed again. She placed the sleeping baby in the crib and exited the bedroom—probably off to tuck in her other kids, Allison thought.

She continued to watch as lights started to go off in the house—first the kitchen light, then the light in the dining room, and a few minutes later Becky reentered the master bedroom and turned off the lamp on the nightstand.

Only one light left. Allison observed Weston as he settled into the couch in the living room to watch television. *You've had a hard week, mister—enjoy the late local news...maybe shut your eyes for a little while.* Allison calculated that she'd give everyone a half hour or so to fall asleep, and then slip over to pay Weston a visit—with a bit of luck she might not even wake the rest of the house. *I'm nothing, if not a considerate killer, though I wish I had my sniper rifle instead of this pistol.*

Allison had considered bringing along her very expensive rifle as a checked bag but decided against it as the authorities were likely to contact the airport, after she'd done the deed, to see if anyone had flown in with a firearm. Likewise, she knew better than to buy a secondhand rifle from a second-rate gun dealer. She could tell if the weapon was in working order at the point of purchase, but without firing it first, she couldn't be certain that its aim was true, and there's nothing more embarrassing for a sniper than a miss.

Besides this job has damn near developed into a vendetta for me, so I want to get in close to really appreciate the kill.

Another patrol car drove past, blocking Allison's line of sight. When it had gone, she cursed to herself as she watched Weston turn off the TV. He rose from the couch and walked to the stairs, switching off the light in the living room.

I've really grown to detest you Weston, but I don't have anything against the kids living in that house. If you make me go upstairs to kill you, things will get messy...so get some sleep mister, and I'll go back to my hotel room to do the same. I'll see you again tomorrow. I imagine we'll each appreciate the moment all the more if we're both well rested.

Chapter 46

Weston checked on Ance and then climbed into bed, covering himself with the comforter and pressing his body against Becky's.

"Your feet are like icicles," she said drowsily.

He rubbed her shoulders. "Some of my parts are cold, and others are warm. Care to guess which?"

"Well, your fingers feel like icicles too."

"Only because touching your body makes all the blood rush from my extremities to a more centralized area."

"Aren't you tired? I figured you'd fall asleep on the couch watching the late-night talk shows the way you usually do."

"Nothing like a brush with death to compel a body to get off of the couch."

"I've been so worried about you this week...you being in the hospital again reminded me of when you got shot."

"Only in the foot...Slim took a lot worse than that, and he's up and about now just like me."

"Because neither of you have sense enough to take cover when people are after you...and he signed up for that sort of thing—he has training and wears body armor. What do you have?"

"The love of a good woman." He caressed her back. "At least I'm hoping so."

"I'm serious. Having you in my life has been such a blessing for me and my boys. I love you so much, but I feel myself worrying all the time that we're going to lose you the way we lost my ex-husband."

"That's a completely different situation...and Rodney is getting better now that he's gotten the help he needs."

"I'm not talking about him; I'm talking about how he made me feel then and how you're making me feel now—sick with worry."

"Everything's going to be fine," he said, "for all of us."

"I don't know if I believe you, but it feels good to hear you say that. What did Slim want when he stopped by earlier?"

"Oh, just to tell me that he was going to have officers driving by the house now and then, but that there wasn't anything to be concerned about."

"That's good to know." She turned toward him. "How do you think things will go with Kate when Edwin drives up to see her tomorrow?"

"It's difficult to predict. Edwin's been my friend for a long time, and I've never heard him once express the least bit of interest in having a relationship, but when I first saw him with Kate last winter he seemed like a totally different person."

"She must see something special in him...and have more patience than Job. After him staying here for just a couple of days, I was ready to send him back to living in the woods."

"It's good that he's leaving H.P.'s place tomorrow. I don't think Edwin would last more than a day at his house."

"It's nice to have him gone and you back." She draped an arm over him.

"Any chance of us having a proper welcome home party tonight?"

"Any chance of you ever rescheduling your colonoscopy appointment?"

"Absolutely...in fact if you and I play doctor right now, it'll be good practice for my exam later."

Chapter 47

H.P. awoke to the sound of music—highly irritating music for so early in the morning. He got out of bed and found Edwin sitting in the middle of the living room floor with papers spread all around him. "What is that noise?"

"It's a recording of theremin music," said Edwin. "It helps me think abstractly."

"That's funny, because a lack of theremin music helps me sleep soundly. What time is it?"

"I don't know...daytime."

H.P. glanced out the window to confirm that Edwin was correct—though only just, given the subtlety of the light. "Have you been at this all night?"

"I tried to sleep, but I'm used to being up at nighttime to observe the stars."

H.P. took a seat on his recliner. "Are you also maybe a little anxious about seeing Kate tomorrow...well, later today?"

"I suppose I might be. This is all unexplored space for me. Weston mentioned that you recently broke up with someone. Any advice for how to talk to an ex-girlfriend?"

"None that's any good, though I'd recommend bringing her something more than a smelly old pizza box."

"That's a sagacious recommendation...perhaps I'll

buy her some flowers. Any idea what sorts of flowers are in season now?"

"No idea whatsoever, but I'm sure she'll like whatever you pick for her."

Edwin nodded. "I appreciate you letting me stay here and borrow your car. Even if mine hadn't been destroyed out at the telescope, I don't think it could've made the trip all the way up to Chicago."

"My car's no great shakes either—especially now that it's covered in scorch marks, but luckily it still runs fine."

"You sure you're not going to need it while I'm gone?"

"No, Weston's coming over around noon with some lunch, and we're going to try to get some more writing done."

"I would never have guessed in an eon that you two would one day collaborate on a book."

H.P. shook his head. "It's not written yet."

"True, but then neither are all the other books that someday will be."

"That's...an interesting perspective."

"Abstract thinking—I'll leave this CD behind, in case you two want to listen to it while you work."

H.P. bobbed his head along with the music. "It is eerily beautiful."

"It always reminds me of looking through my first telescope...here comes my favorite series of glissandos."

Chapter 48

Allison wanted to keep as low a profile as possible, so she forwent her morning run, thinking that the sight of a woman with scars covering half her face out for a jog might be memorable to a passerby. And since she didn't have her usual check-in call, her morning was atypically open. She flipped through the channels on her room's television, from the inane morning talk shows to reruns of old sitcoms she couldn't imagine people enjoying in their heyday.

How do housewives do it? But then Allison thought of all the times her sister, a homemaker herself, complained of never having a free moment, and so she figured there was probably more to it than watching TV and making sandwiches.

As she sat in bed, she considered ordering room service for breakfast, but she didn't find anything on the menu to be terribly tantalizing—all easy-make items probably whipped up by someone who doubled as a housekeeper just so the hotel could claim to offer room service. Then the same copulatory cacophony started again from next door that had kept her up half the night, discovering only after calling down to the front desk to complain that her room was adjacent to the honeymoon suite. *I suppose that's how you know you're staying in a classy hotel—the fornicating is done by married people.*

She took her flip phone off the nightstand and

called one of her contacts.

"Hello," a deep voice answered.

"Hey, did your snake ever turn up?"

"Kelly, is that you?"

"You bet, my pet."

"I'm glad you called. Yeah, Mister Slither was hiding in the kitchen cabinet behind my containers of creatine powder the whole time."

"Naughty python, always hiding in the last place you look."

"That's the weird thing—I open that cabinet several times a day."

"So then maybe he crawled in there just before you found him and had been hiding somewhere else earlier."

"Huh, I hadn't thought of that."

Shocking. "I'm glad you two are reunited. I always enjoy a *tail* with a happy ending."

"The way you said 'tail'...you made a pun, didn't you?"

"I know how much you enjoy them, precious."

"I haven't seen you at the bar lately. Has everything been okay?"

Allison let out a long sigh. "Not really, but I don't want to bother you with my troubles."

"It's no bother or trouble...you listened to me when I was broken up about my snake. Tell me what's going on with you."

"Well, I got into a horrible car crash—sideswiped by this distracted driver...and to make matters worse, now he refuses to pay for my medical bills, even though the wreck was totally his fault."

Chapter 49

H.P. was reading an out-of-date pop-culture magazine on his front porch when Weston pulled up. Weston got out of his car with a pizza box in hand.

"You've got to be kidding me," said H.P.

"What…it's not from the same pizzeria, and I picked it up myself. If you drank one poisoned cup of coffee, you wouldn't stop drinking all coffee forever."

"I might."

"The hair of the dog that bit you, my friend."

"You know that doesn't actually work, right? Not for rabies, hangovers, or poisonings."

Weston stepped onto the porch with the pizza. "There's a first time for everything."

"Not necessarily…for instance, there never has been and never will be a first time to celebrate the Fourth of July in June."

"Fine—you got me, you pedantic contrarian. Now do you want some lunch or not?"

"Sure, let's eat out here. The sun feels good."

Weston set the pizza on a small wooden table in front of two wicker chairs, while H.P. went inside and soon returned with plates, napkins, and a couple of glasses of iced tea.

Weston grudgingly accepted a glass of tea. "I see that I should've brought some beer too."

"Oh, I've got beer inside, and you can have one

just as soon as we get the first couple of pages written."

"You're a taskmaster...no wonder your students can't stand you."

As Weston devoured his first slice, H.P. cautiously took a piece and inspected it before taking a bite.

"Did Edwin leave early this morning?" Weston asked with a full mouth.

"Very early...we had a little heart-to-heart before he left."

"Better you than me."

"Do you think she'll help us."

"Kate...yeah, I'm sure she will. What I don't know is whether it'll matter."

H.P. eyed Weston quizzically. "How do you mean?"

"You experienced the drug's effects too...what I described to the doctors about my trip seemed to them rather singular, meaning that whatever this drug is, there's probably not much out there that's like it, which I suspect will make it difficult to trace back to a potential manufacturer, who undoubtedly went to great lengths to cover their tracks. I think the best we can hope for is that Edwin makes a love connection...but then I could be wrong. Like I told you before, there's a first time for everything."

"I hope you are wrong...both for obvious reasons and because it's difficult to be friends with someone who's always right. You raise an interesting point, though—with all our running around yesterday, I didn't have a chance to ask...what was your 'trip' like?"

"Are you asking me if I saw blue mice and pink elephants?"

"I'm asking if you saw any of your characters...did

you happen to have a chat with your Spinster?"

"I knew it!" Weston stamped his feet. "Middle-aged novelists don't just out of nowhere write a manuscript so completely different from all the other books in their long-running series. Your drug trip was the journey you described in your latest Pirate Hunter installment, wasn't it?"

"I'll answer your question, if you answer mine first."

Chapter 50

Allison and her bodybuilder companion sat in the rental car across the road from H.P.'s farmhouse after having tailed Weston there.

"Whose house is that?" he asked. "The guy that crashed into you?"

She peered through her binoculars. "No, my pet...remember the guy we were following was the one who hit me."

"But his car didn't look damaged."

That's actually a good point. "He was driving a different car then...it's probably still in the shop. Maybe the car he's driving now belongs to the guy who lives here, since I don't see another vehicle in the driveway, though it's hard to tell for sure with all the trees blocking my view."

"That makes sense—if he's too cheap to pay your medical bills, then he's probably too cheap to pay for a rental car like you." Allison always appreciated when her dupes filled in their own blanks—made the story hold together better. "What do you want me to do...go over there and convince him to pay up?"

Allison looked him over as she weighed her options. The bodybuilder wasn't the big bruiser that Brent had been, but though smaller in stature he possessed a formidable physique. *I suspect this is H.P.'s place, but I can barely see the house through all*

185

the foliage. I could send muscle head here over to do some reconnaissance, but he might spook them...not to mention that recon most likely isn't his forte.

"I've got a plan." Allison grabbed her raincoat off the backseat. "Why don't you get out and put this on?"

The bodybuilder took her raincoat and exited the car as she rummaged around for some other items: the bag her drive-thru breakfast had come in for subterfuge, the empty cardboard box that had contained her egg sandwich for volume, and several folded maps for weight.

He walked to the driver's side of the car wearing her raincoat. Allison thought it looked tight in the arms, but that it had enough roominess in the middle to hide his barrel chest.

"It's not even raining," he said.

Allison got out of her car with the bag from the fast-food restaurant. "I know, precious, but it gives you an official look."

"So what's the plan?"

"First, we need to figure out what the situation is over there. We don't want to strongarm this guy if he's attending some kid's birthday party, right?"

"Yeah, that wouldn't be good."

"No, it wouldn't." Allison handed him the bag. "I want you to take this sack and drive on over to the house. Act like you're a delivery guy who's lost. Scope out the scene while you're there—see how many people are around and what they're doing."

"What do I tell them if they ask me the address I'm looking for?"

I think his snake tried to leave home because it figured out that it was smarter than its owner. "Just make something up."

"I could say my own address."

"Well, that's not made up, is it, pet?" Allison patted his shoulder. "But the important thing is that you don't dillydally—drive right back here and report what you saw, and then I'll figure out our next play from there."

Chapter 51

Weston was about to answer H.P.'s question when he noticed a car pulling up the long driveway. "Are you expecting someone?"

"Nope," H.P. answered, "and almost no one ever just drops by all the way out here."

"It only looks like one guy, so I don't think we have anything to worry about, but if he should try something, you tackle him, and I'll go run for help."

The car parked behind Weston's. A man wearing a raincoat and holding a paper bag with a fast-food logo got out. "I'm a delivery driver...did you guys order some lunch?"

"No," Weston shouted from the front porch. "As you can see, we're already eating lunch."

"What address are you looking for?" asked H.P.

"Uh...is this Main Street?"

"Are you asking if my driveway is Main Street?"

"No...I mean the road back there."

"Main Street goes through the middle of town," H.P. said. "Out here the roads just have numbers for names."

"Okay—I think I got turned around someplace, so I'll just head back to town now."

Weston looked at H.P. "That was odd."

"I think it's about to get odder still."

A pickup truck pulled into the driveway and

parked, blocking in the ersatz delivery vehicle. Slim stepped out and flashed his police badge. "Hang on there a moment."

"What's the problem, Officer?"

"I'll ask the questions." Slim approached the man with the bag, eyeing his car along the way. "What are you doing out here?"

"I'm a delivery driver, and I got lost…I deliver food, and this is getting cold, so—"

Slim took note of the man's coat. "You drive for Rainy Day Delivery?"

"Yeah…that's right."

"Don't it eat into your profits to make your deliveries with a rental car?"

"My car's in the shop…got sideswiped, so I'm just using this one for now."

"Okay, last question." Slim pointed to the bag the driver held. "What's in there?"

"I don't know…I just pick them up and drop them off."

"Well, then open it up."

"Like I told you, this food is getting cold, so I really need to—"

Slim snatched the bag out of the man's hand. "If you drove all the way out here from town, then this food has been cold for a while now." He examined the contents of the bag. "What kind of lunch is an empty box and a bunch of maps?"

"I…I don't know," the man stammered. "Maybe there was a mix up at the restaurant."

"Until we get this mix up squared away, I want you to sit up in the cab of my truck. You ain't under arrest yet, but I'm going to put some handcuffs on you just the same."

****

Slim ended the call on his mobile phone and then climbed the front porch stairs to talk with H.P. and Weston. "Okay, the skinny is that he's a part-time personal trainer, part-time bouncer, and zero-time delivery driver, so I can arrest him for giving a false statement to a police officer, but if he didn't make any threats or cause any trouble—that's about it."

"No trouble," H.P. said, "he seemed more hapless than anything."

"Did he tell you if he knew our gal?" asked Weston.

"You saw me try to interrogate him after I got him in the truck. Once the cuffs went on his mouth went shut. That's how it goes sometimes—probably the smartest move he's made in a while."

Weston shrugged. "So what should we do?"

"What you should've done is what I told you to do last night. Keep your head down, which doesn't involve driving all around, making yourself a moving target. If you stay put at Becky's, I can make sure you're safe. I stopped by her house to check on you, and she told me you drove all the way over here."

"I thought you told me there was nothing to be concerned about."

"I told you there was probably nothing to be concerned about, provided you stay in one place where I can keep an eye on you."

Weston nodded. "Oh...well, you should've made that point clearer."

"Then let me make it real clear to you right now— go back to Becky's and stay there. I don't know what all this was, but it don't smell right. I'm going to drop the idget sitting in my truck off at the station for booking, then swap out my pickup for a patrol car and come straight over to Becky's to campout in her driveway, and you damn well better be there when I show up."

"Okay Slim—jeez—I'm going...no need to blow a fuse."

"H.P., I don't think whoever's after him is necessarily after you, but now that it seems likely that they know where you live, I'd feel a whole lot better if you bunked at Becky's too...at least for the next few days."

"Sure, that makes sense," said H.P. "I'll just go grab a few things."

Weston stood up and stretched. "Since it seems we're having a protracted sleepover, you might as well bring along Edwin's sleeping bag too. I know Becky will be thrilled to have him back."

Chapter 52

Weston loaded up the trunk of his car with two sleeping bags, half a case of wine, a box of papers, and a suitcase as H.P. put his messenger bag on the front seat.

"You sure that's everything?" Weston asked sardonically.

H.P. climbed his front porch steps. "No actually, I should doublecheck that the backdoor is locked and grab Edwin's theremin CD."

"What the hell kind of music is that?"

"We'll play it in the car...I'm sure you'll hate it."

Weston grumbled to himself as he rearranged the items in his trunk so that the six wine bottles wouldn't shift around in transit. "Why would I want to listen to music that you think I'll hate? You don't know, maybe I'll like this three-minute music...my tastes are eclectic. I'm opened minded, damnit."

Weston closed his trunk lid to see a woman walking out of the house, holding a gun to H.P.'s head. Weston studied her face as she studied him.

"H.P., you mentioned this old farmhouse had ghosts, but you never told me they were so scary looking. A face like that could frighten Stevie Wonder. Allison, I presume."

"Oh Weston, you just don't know when to shut up." Allison slowly walked H.P. down the porch steps.

"My plan had been to say hello, just so you knew it was me, and then goodbye, shooting you straight away— quick and easy, but you had to open your mouth, so now I have a new plan.

****

Weston and H.P. wriggled in an attempt to free themselves from the duct tape restraining them in a seated position against the barn's central support beam as Allison searched the recesses of the dilapidated outbuilding.

"I can hear you two struggling to get loose," Allison called from the back of the barn. "I don't blame you for trying to escape, but if you do manage to tear through that tape, I'll just shoot you in the back as you run away."

"She's a mean one," H.P. whispered.

"Hell hath no fury like a woman scarred," said Weston.

Allison approached with a gas can in hand. "What are you boys whispering about?"

"He was wondering why someone like you becomes a hitwoman in the first place," Weston answered. "I figure it's because of your name, Allison Belched. The kids at school must've teased you mercilessly."

"So how is it that you know my name?"

"If you let us go, I'll tell you," replied Weston.

"Since you know my name, I have all the more reason to kill you...not that I needed any. It doesn't really matter anyway. I was going to change my face, so I may as well change my identity while I'm at it."

"Might I suggest Allison Burped?" asked Weston.

"Or perhaps Allison Eructed?" added H.P.

Weston nodded. "Oh, that does have a nice ring to it."

"I'm so pleased you two are enjoying yourselves," Allison said. "Laughter now, and then screaming later...though much sooner than later."

"So what do you have in mind for our demise?" H.P. eyed the container she held. "Are you going to beat us to death with an empty gas can?"

"Yeah, what's with this place? I saw this old barn as I was circling around through the woods while you two were chatting with that cop I shot, and I thought to myself, 'That looks like a good spot for a gruesome death.' But now that we're here I discover that there's no hay in the loft to set on fire, no farming implements with which to thresh your skin from your bones...the only useful thing I found is this gas can, and there's nothing in it."

"I cleared everything out when I first moved in. I didn't want anything in here that was flammable, and I gave all the farming equipment away to people I thought could actually use it. This barn is pretty much a bird sanctuary now...sorry to disappoint."

Allison studied the walls of the barn. "Oh, I'm not disappointed. This old wood is plenty flammable, and I can just siphon some gas out of my rental car."

Weston shook his head. "I wouldn't do that if I were you. If you return a rental on empty, those places will charge you an arm and a leg."

Allison smiled. "I'll be glad to give them yours, Weston...at least the ashes. You know, it wasn't the glass that exploded into my face that hurt the most—it was the burns."

"I was about to offer that you could siphon the gas

from my car instead," said Weston, "but now I take it back."

"To think I came all the way down here just to plug you full of holes. What a missed opportunity that would've been, when a weenie roast will be so much more delicious."

"That's an odd euphemism, isn't it?" asked H.P. "To 'plug someone full of holes'...it seems to me that shooting somebody would cause holes rather than plug them, but then I suppose unplugging somebody full of holes doesn't sound quite right either."

"H.P., I'll miss our little chats. I read one of your books on the flight here; the Pirate Hunter is a terrific character, and I've got nothing against you personally, but then—fair or not—we're judged by the company we keep. I'm truly sorry you got caught up in all this, for whatever it's worth."

"It'd be worth a whole lot if you'd reconsider your present course of action and see fit to let us go," said H.P. "Please?"

"I guess I'm not really that sorry after all. You two do make quite a pair, tied up as you are and moments away from burning to death—the adventure writer who's afraid to die, and the romance writer who's afraid to love...or at least marry his baby's mama."

"That's what we writers do," said Weston. "We tell lies from left to right in order to make ourselves feel better about who we really are, which is why writers have no secrets—we use up all our dishonesty on the page. But then who are you to cast aspersions at me about not tying the knot? I noticed you've got quite an engagement ring there but no wedding band to match."

Allison glanced at her ring finger. "Who has time

to get married these days? Besides, it's not a real engagement ring. I mean it's a real diamond, but I bought it myself—cost me a fortune…had to kill a politician to afford it."

Weston frowned. "Where has all the romance gone?"

"Up in smoke, I suspect…just like you two soon will. Okay boys, we've had some laughs, but now it's time to bid you adieu."

With that Allison took the gas can and left, closing the barndoor behind her.

H.P. started struggling again to break free of the duct tape. "What do you want to talk about?"

"What do you mean, what do I want to talk about?" Weston also fought to free himself from the tape.

"You know, now that we're immured…like my idea for our story."

"I'm not worried about being immured right now, I'm worried about being immolated. Anyway, we're not immured, we're trapped in a barn."

"We're enclosed within walls—that means we're immured."

"Then let's see about getting unimmured. Can you stand?"

"I can try."

Weston strained to rise to his feet. "All right, then do it."

"You don't want to do a three count?"

"We don't have time for that."

"I think it might help to facilitate our standing up together, you know, like a rocket launch."

"Should I count backwards then?" Weston asked.

"Just count!"

"Fine, one...two...three."

Weston and H.P. pushed upward but failed to achieve liftoff and unceremoniously slid the short distance back down to the ground.

Weston exhaled heavily. "Wow, she really likes to use a lot of tape."

"Do you have a pocketknife you could try cutting it with?"

"I do, but—wouldn't you know it—the damn thing is in my pocket, and my hands are bound together. Can you try fishing it out?"

"No, my hands are taped too."

"Are they really, or do you just not feel comfortable reaching into another man's pocket?" asked Weston. "Because now's not the time for shyness."

"My hands are really taped, and also I really don't feel comfortable doing that."

"On a positive note, if we don't make it out of this, then we won't have to write that book."

"I always pretty much figured that was never actually going to work."

"Why didn't you say so?"

"I don't know," said H.P. "It seemed important to you, so I thought it at least worth a try."

"Sure, I thought it was a good idea at first, but it's not like I would've been crushed if you'd told me no."

"Then for the record I'm telling you no, now. My experiences with you of late have shown me that life is just too short."

"Great, now what do I have to live for? Oh, and by the way, begging for our lives was very poor form."

"I didn't beg for our lives," H.P. replied. "I simply

asked her if she might reconsider."

"No, I think it was begging."

Allison's face appeared in a gap between two boards in the barn wall. "Reluctantly, I have to agree with Weston. It was that sad little 'please' at the end that made it begging."

"I'm offended by the accuracy of these comments," H.P. said.

"All right boys, I trust you've made your peace with being burned alive like John Wilkes Booth." Allison began to splash gasoline against the outside of the barn.

"Wasn't he shot before he burned in that barn?" asked H.P.

"Don't give her any ideas. Besides, she's from Canada—she probably knows way more about American history than you and I put together know about Canadian history."

"But if she's Canadian, why isn't she nicer?" H.P. looked over his shoulder as best he could. "What's happening? I can't see her anymore."

"She's on my side now. That can holds a lot more gas than I would've thought."

"Has she lit it yet?"

"Not yet...no hang on, she just did. This old wood looks pretty dry. I bet it'll burn fast."

"Probably, but I imagine the roof will collapse and crush us to death before the fire ever reaches us...or maybe the fumes will get us first."

"Ever the optimist, you are."

"Why are you still talking and not screaming?" Allison shouted at Weston.

"She really is a vindictive one," said Weston.

"She certainly scares the hell out of me. It must be that effect you have on women you told me about."

"I'm going to start shooting kneecaps if I don't hear some screams," Allison yelled over the crackling flames.

"Help," screamed H.P. "Oh, won't someone help us?"

"I want Weston to scream—not you, H.P. Besides, that was some pathetic screaming."

"She's right about that," Weston said. "You've turned in just an all-around pitiful performance today."

"Last chance, Weston. Who knows, from out here I might miss your kneecap and shoot you someplace even more sensitive."

"Do your worst, witch," Weston yelled back.

The loud report of a gunshot rang out.

"Weston, are you okay? Why did you have to incite her like that? Where are you shot?"

"I...I don't think I am," Weston answered.

"You mean she missed?"

"I mean I don't think it was her who fired that shot."

"Why do you say that?"

Weston stared between the boards for a moment at Allison's body slumped against the outer wall of the barn. "Because I think she's dead."

"Are you sure?"

"Pretty sure...she's not moving even though her shirt's on fire, and it looks like half her face is missing—though I suppose on the plus side, it's the half that was already messed up."

"So then we're out of danger?"

"We're still trapped in a burning barn, and

someone is shooting in our general direction, so I wouldn't say we're out of danger yet."

"Who fired the shot?"

Weston squinted to get a better look at a figure in the distance. "Uhm…I don't think you'd believe me if I told you."

"Try me."

"Just keep in mind that we're currently in a highly stressful situation, and it's hard to see between the boards and through the flames…but uh, I think bigfoot shot her."

"Are you high on drugs again?"

"If I'm not, I wish I were, but yep…bigfoot just walked out of the woods carrying a rifle, and he's headed this way."

H.P. attempted to look over his shoulder again. "What in the world are you talking about?"

"I'll stop telling you what I see if you want me to, but that's not going to keep me from seeing it."

"What's happening now?"

"He's almost to the barn…he just picked up Allison's body…and, uh oh, I think I'm going to lose my lunch—there went the other half of her head."

Weston managed to keep his lunch down as a tall figure, who did indeed resemble bigfoot, slid open the barndoor.

"Oh, that explains it." H.P. coughed. "It's a guy in a ghillie suit."

"What the hell is a ghillie suit?"

"You know…a big, camouflage outfit snipers wear to blend in with the foliage of their environment. The Pirate Hunter has a couple of them in his wardrobe."

"I'd find that fascinating if not for the menacing

fellow coming toward us carrying a dead body over his shoulder and a large knife in his hand."

The camouflaged man dropped Allison's headless corpse on the ground at their feet and then raised his knife above them. He adroitly slashed at the duct tape, quickly cutting them lose. They both stared up at the imposing figure.

"Now would be a good time to leave," said the sniper.

Weston and H.P. did just that with the camouflaged man following them out of the barn. Once outside and away from the burning barn, the two middle-aged writers fell to the ground, gasping for fresh air.

"Sorry, fellas, I would've been here sooner, but I had a difficult time tracking her car's GPS through the rental agency's janky app."

H.P. took a deep breath. "Are you an employee of the rental agency?"

The sniper smiled. "No, I work for…an association. I'm the guy they dispatch when one of our associates goes rogue and…well, needs to be dispatched. Which one of you is Weston?"

"That's me." Weston coughed. "Unless you intend to shoot me, in which case it's him."

The sniper grinned again. He pulled out an envelope from underneath the collar of his suit and stuffed it into Weston's shirt pocket. "It's a note from the client that contracted my association. Enjoy the rest of your day, gentlemen."

Weston and H.P. watched as the camouflaged man walked without another word back into the woods. Then they heard a crashing sound and turned to see the barn's roof collapse, sending flames and smoke higher into the air.

"What does the note read?"

Weston took the envelope from his shirt pocket, opened it, unfolded the piece of paper within, and then read it aloud.

" 'Our organization has recently undergone a restructuring of upper management, and during that process the decision was made to cease all our operations in your area as it's been determined that they don't merit the exposure. Moreover, no further attempts will be made on your life, as it's been determined that you don't merit the expenditure.' "

"No signature from your secret admirer?"

"Nope, it seems the party that sent this wishes to remain anonymous."

H.P. let out a deep breath. "I suppose we could tell the story, just to let the world know they're out there."

"Yes, I suppose we could, though who would ever believe an adventure author and a romance writer?"

The two sat contemplatively in the tall grass, watching the barn burn.

Chapter 53

H.P. set up the card table in his living room, while Weston peeled the cellophane from a new deck of playing cards. Edwin poured three glasses of water and handed one to H.P. and another to Weston. Then he passed out the pills.

"Should someone make a toast?" Edwin asked.

"It's bad luck to toast with water," H.P. said.

"It can't be any worse than toasting with laxatives." Weston raised his glass. "Here's to what will undoubtedly go down in history as the crappiest bachelor party of all time." The three clinked their glasses and swallowed their pills. "Seriously though, I appreciate you two agreeing to get colonoscopies with me tomorrow."

"It's the most peculiar groomsmen gift I've ever heard of," said Edwin, "but I'm glad we'll be there to offer support."

H.P. shook his head. "I think this is more about misery loving company than support, but since it's the only way Becky would agree to marry him, I'm pleased to be of *ass*-istance."

Edwin scratched his beard. "It seems somewhat unfair that we groomsmen are made to share in this unpleasant task before the happy event, whereas the best man gets off scot-free."

"That's true," Weston replied. "As he's quite a few

years younger than us, he's off the hook for now, but he'll get his in the end."

Edwin nodded. "I suppose we all do eventually— that is if we're fortunate enough to live so long."

"Should we start playing poker or wait for Slim?" H.P. asked.

Weston sat down at the card table. "Let's get started. He sometimes gets hung up on paperwork at the end of his shift."

H.P. took a seat. "Speaking of shift, don't forget about the downstairs bathroom, if the one up here should happen to be occupied."

Weston dealt the cards. "Let's start with five card draw...Bloody Marys wild."

Edwin joined them at the table. "Which ones are those again?"

"Red queens," H.P. answered, "hearts and diamonds."

Edwin examined his cards. "That reminds me, I was over at Becky's the other day getting the last of my gear from her garage, and I noticed the diamond ring you gave her Weston—that's quite a rock. Looked similar to another engagement ring I saw not so long ago, though the setting was different."

"The stone was a gift from H.P.," said Weston.

Edwin raised an eyebrow. "That's a very generous gift."

H.P. reordered the cards in his hand. "Not really...it didn't cost me anything. It's amazing what you can turn up when digging around in your own backyard."

Weston glanced up from his cards. "Edwin, you've been spending so much time upstate that we've hardly seen you of late. Will you be bringing Kate to the wedding? I recall how fond she is of seeing you in a tuxedo."

"Yes, I believe I will. By the way, Kate wanted me to let you two know that she was finally able to isolate the compound contained in the grease on that pizza box you had me take to her. She and her colleagues didn't recognize the molecular structure, so there's not much chance of tracing it to the manufacturer; however, she did upload the structural formula to the World Health Organization's database for illicit drugs, so they'll be on the lookout for it or a derivative."

"Great, WHO cares," Weston remarked unsarcastically, "let's play some cards." Headlights shined through the front windows, interrupting the first round of betting. "That must be Slim."

Soon someone knocked at the front door.

"It's open," called H.P.

Slim entered with a case of sports drinks. "This stuff is good for keeping you hydrated, though it's not the sort of beverage I usually bring to a bachelor party."

"That's mighty thoughtful of you," said Edwin.

"You're still more than welcome to join us tomorrow morning," added H.P.

"I appreciate the offer, but I've got a few more years of driving to do before I need the full fifty-thousand-mile inspection."

Weston pointed to the vacant chair at the table. "We just started playing five-card draw. Want me to deal you in?"

Slim sat down. "Sure, playing poker tonight seems like a good way to pass the time until you boys get poked tomorrow. This has to be the strangest bachelor party I've ever been to, but Weston, I'm honored that you asked me to be one of your groomsmen, and I can't think of a better choice than who you picked to be your best man."

Chapter 54

Edwin and H.P. struggled to pull on their tuxedo coats in the chapel's basement among the stacks of chairs and decorations for various religious holidays.

"These rental jackets don't offer much in the way of elbow room," said H.P.

"I'm less concerned about my elbows and more concerned that I won't be able to button this damn thing over my belly." Edwin turned his attention to Slim, who was attempting to stomp his feet into a pair of glossy dress shoes. "And look at him...he could practically swim inside that suit."

"They don't call him Slim for nothing."

"Yeah, my tux fits okay," said Slim, "but these damn shoes are harder to get on than a new pair of boots. I told the lady at the rental shop what size I wear."

"They're probably the right size," replied H.P. "You just need a shoehorn. Here—use mine."

Slim accepted the small piece of plastic from H.P. "This don't look like no horn I've ever seen."

"Stick it in the back of the shoe and then slide your heel down into it."

Slim did as H.P. instructed, and his foot slid easily into the shoe. "Well, I'll be...that's a pretty neat trick. You don't happen to have a horn to help me with this here bowtie, do you?"

"I can help you in a minute after I finish tying his." Weston stood in front of a cheval mirror with Van, fussing with the boy's bowtie. "These things are hard enough to tie when you're wearing them. I've never had to tie someone else's before."

"I appreciate you asking me to be your best man and all," Van said, "but now that your wedding day is actually here, I'm having second thoughts."

"About me marrying your mom...I hope you're not starting to have misgivings. It's important to me that you're okay with this. I want you to know that I'll take good care of your mom and her kids, but I'm not trying to replace your dad."

"No, I understand all that...and I'm fine with you marrying my mom—even though we don't always get along, I know that you're a good guy. It's the best man speech afterward at the reception that I'm nervous about."

"But I've heard you practice that speech about a half dozen times now. You'll do great."

"Yeah, it sounded okay in the living room when I was wearing jeans and a sweatshirt, but soon I'll have to give it in this monkey suit in front of a bunch of people I don't know. Can you have H.P. give the speech instead? He's used to talking in front of people."

"I'm sure he'd be glad to have the opportunity to get back at me for the last time I gave a speech in his honor, but me and your mom are really looking forward to hearing you give it. However, we also want you to enjoy the day, so if you don't feel up to it, I can ask H.P. to step in."

"You wouldn't demote me to ring bearer, would you?"

"And take away your brother's job...though I'm sure you could help Ance and your aunt with the flower girl duties." An expression of mortification flashed across Van's face as Weston finished tying his bowtie. "I'm only teasing. I want you standing there right next to me when your mom walks down the aisle...as for the speech, think it over. But you know, making a public address is the only time when it's acceptable to imagine everybody naked."

"Weston," H.P. called. "Come here—I want to see you."

Weston walked over to join his groomsmen.

H.P. nodded to the others. "If that doesn't settle it, then I don't know what will."

"Settle what?" asked Weston.

"H.P. has been trying to convince us that you played Watson to his Sherlock during your recent adventures," Edwin answered. "It seems my role was Mycroft."

"And apparently I'm Inspector Lestrade," added Slim. "I don't know who that is, but as long as he's not some caricature of blundering police incompetence then I'm okay with it."

H.P. crossed his arms. "And to confirm that you are in fact Watson, I called you over here with the same phrase Alexander Graham Bell said to his assistant Watson during the very first telephone conversation...and just as he did, you came right over."

Weston smiled. "While I admit that's interesting, it hardly settles anything. It's but a mere coincidence that has no bearing on your position. By that line of reasoning, the fact that you and John H. Watson share an initial in your name, which also both happen to stand for—"

"Stop right there," interrupted H.P. "I didn't realize you knew what my H stood for, but I'll thank you not to go broadcasting it."

"I see no reason to be piggish with the information," said Weston, "but if you prefer to keep your name to yourself, then I'll respect your wish; however, as for your ham-handed argument, I'm afraid I cannot concede the point."

H.P. signaled Edwin. "I thought you might be too conceited to concede, but nevertheless we'd like to present you with a present both to celebrate your wedding day as well as the positive results of our colonoscopies, which thankfully all turned out negative."

Edwin handed Weston a hatbox. "The salesperson told us that these are made of the finest tweed."

Weston removed the lid from the large box to find five deerstalker hats stacked within. "I can't imagine a clearer instance of, 'if it requires a salesperson to sell it, then you definitely shouldn't buy it.' "

"Put one on," said Slim.

"The bill goes in the front," added Edwin.

H.P. pointed to Van. "We got one for you too, young man. Come on over and try it on."

Van approached as the four men donned their ridiculous hats. "You know what, I've got a long life ahead of me, and I don't want it ruined by anyone seeing me wear one of those things...but they look great on you guys. Huddle up and let me snap a pic."

Slim, Edwin, Weston, and H.P. stood shoulder to shoulder as Van took a photo with his smartphone.

"I assume we appear distinguished in our tuxes and

tweed," H.P. said.

Van studied the screen of his phone. "Yes, very *dick*-nified."

"Would you send that picture to all of us?" asked Weston.

"Oh, don't worry. I'll for sure be sending this pic out to everybody I know, but just so all the people at the wedding can see this in person, I'll make you a deal. Wear those hats at the reception, and I'll give the best man speech...there's nothing I could say that would be more embarrassing than how you all look."

A word about the author...

Wesley Payton has a B.A. in Rhetoric/Philosophy and an M.A. in English. He has been a short-story presenter for the Illinois Philological Association. His play *Way Station* was selected for a Next Draft reading in 2015, and *What Does a Question Weigh?* was selected for a staged reading as part of the 2017 Chicago New Work Festival. He is the author of the novels *Lead Tears*, *Darkling Spinster*, *Darkling Spinster No More*, *Standing in Doorways*, *Raison Deidre*, *Oblong*, *Intimate Recreation*, and *The House Painter and the Pirate Hunter*. Wesley and his family live in Oak Park, Illinois.

Weston and H.P. will appear next in *Dissimiles: More's the Pity*.

Find out more about Wesley and his books here: http://wespayton.weebly.com/

CPSIA information can be obtained
at www.ICGtesting.com
Printed in the USA
LVHW052124290122
709481LV00013B/373

9 781509 239153